The Show

The Show

A Novel by Filip Syta

Sex. Drugs. Tech.
Silicon Valley—the new Wall Street.

INKSHARES

Published by Inkshares, Inc., San Francisco, California
www.inkshares.com

Edited and designed by Girl Friday Productions
www.girlfridayproductions.com

Front cover design by Cristopher Benitah
Full cover design by David Drummond

ISBN: 9781941758151
eISBN: 9781941758243
Library of Congress Control Number: 2015938849

First edition

Printed in the United States of America

This work of passion is dedicated to you.

PART 1

1

I could feel the blood pressure in my veins; it dropped a notch after the dinging sound. The fasten seat belt sign went off, and the plane was now cruising at thirty-five thousand feet toward my new life.

I could barely wait to get there and meet the people already on the inside, the ones who'd made it. I was on my way to a new life in the rapidly growing tech industry, which was shaping the world after its own agenda. By working at the most powerful tech company in the world, SHOW, I would help shape that agenda.

It meant I now belonged to the best of the best. I would rub shoulders with the elite and be part of changing the world for the better. I was a dreamer. Although SHOW's main business was online advertising, they were aiming for the stars, and so was I.

"Hi there, sir. Coffee or tea?" asked the flight attendant.

She smiled like it was her birthday, but her eyes looked stressed and angry. Her hair was messy, and I had never seen a woman blink as fast as she did. Maybe the clumps of mascara on the lashes of her left eye bothered her.

"Whiskey on the rocks," I answered, giving her an even bigger smile.

"Sorry, sir, we're out of ice."

"Already? Must have been some thirsty folks in the front rows."

"Broken ice machine," she replied quickly.

"Then I'll have the whiskey without the rocks, please."

The lady in the leather seat on my left followed the glass with her eyes as the flight attendant leaned over her to hand me the drink. The flight attendant was no longer trying to smile. Her painted red lips made her seem like a sad clown that nobody was laughing at.

I took a sip of my straight Jack and gazed out the small round window at the clouds. They looked like soft cotton candy. Whenever I fly, I imagine how it would feel to walk out on the wingtip, step down, and stroll around on that cloudy cotton candy field with a drink in my hand while looking down at the world to see what humanity is doing. This time, I felt closer to the clouds than ever. I felt like a rock star, like someone more than special. I felt like God herself.

I decided to celebrate that feeling with another whiskey and pressed the "Service" button. The lady next to me glanced at me nervously. A few minutes later, the flight attendant was pouring more Jack into my glass. I examined her closely, wondering why she was doing this job. For some reason, her eyes made me think of a sleepy koala bear that had overdosed on eucalyptus and was as high as the Empire State Building. She clearly didn't enjoy her work, so why did she do it? Why not have a career you love? Like the one I was headed toward. Maybe she had no choice. Maybe she had a kid to support and her husband had left her for another woman—or man. What a sad and miserable woman, wasting her life up in the sky serving Jack. At least the view was good.

My blood pressure skyrocketed, and I knew it was time. The fasten seat belt sign went on, and the plane started its descent toward the city of innovation, the city from which the world was being reshaped: San Francisco.

I chugged my whiskey as the lady next to me gave me a disappointed stare, the look she probably gave her drunk husband during Christmas dinner.

"Cheers!" I said loudly and buckled up.

The show was about to start, and I was certain it would be a good one.

2

I woke up in the middle of the night and looked around the room in a panic, trying to remember where I was. I was staying at the Hyatt, and the bed was so pillowy that I was afraid I'd drown in the mattress and miss my first day of work. I started to think about the clouds I'd seen through the airplane window, and I imagined they were my bed. As I came to my senses, I found the TV remote and flipped through a few channels, all showing reruns of shitty sitcoms from the late nineties.

I thought about the miserable flight attendant and her red lips, wondering if she could sleep. Maybe she was having martinis with the captain, searching for happiness. Maybe not. I didn't really care. I sank back into the mattress and fell asleep.

I woke up again around six thirty, fought my way out of the squishy bed, and went to the bathroom. I checked myself out in the mirror and observed my facial hair for a couple of minutes before I started to shave. The disposable razor I'd bought at Ralphs back home in Los Angeles the other day was dull, making the experience slightly different from the TV commercials in which they get the perfect shave every single time. There was no fresh and cool feeling, no smooth, perfect skin, and definitely no sexy woman wiping my face with a clean, soft white cotton towel.

After a lousy shaving job, I showered and washed my hair using the tiny bottle of shampoo from the hotel bathroom. The white towel provided had clearly been washed too many times; it felt like sandpaper. I put my underwear on, combed my hair, and took out a blue shirt from my bag. I put it on without ironing it. It was wrinkled but good enough. In the tech world, you're supposed to have an "I don't give a fuck" attitude anyway, or so I'd read in magazines. I liked the fact that I didn't have to become a suit guy like my friends who worked in corporate banking. I looked in the mirror and listened to "You're the Best" by Joe Esposito on my iPhone while I eye-fucked myself.

This was it—they'd get what they'd get. I was ready to stride into that office and become a part of history. I was excited and proud and, at the same time, scared as fuck.

I left my room, took the elevator down to the lobby, and ventured out to the street. The sunlight was barely making it through the cloudy skies, and the fresh October breeze turned my combed hair into a wild bush.

It was Monday morning, and people on Market Street were struggling against the wind with determined steps—time for another week of work, another week of responsibilities. I kept going with a smile. On that Monday some cold wind would not mess with my mood.

After a twenty-minute walk southeast along Second Street toward South Park and Townsend Street, I saw it: the tall black building in which I would now spend my working days. I stopped for a moment to stare at it, and the hair on my arms stood like the quills of a scared hedgehog. The headquarters of SHOW. I could almost smell the success and innovation, the billions of dollars passing through the building. I started to move again, and my heart pounded faster and faster the closer I got. Once outside the main entrance, I checked that my fly was closed and dragged my hand through my messy hair. I glanced at the silver watch on my left arm, which I'd gotten from my father as a gift just four months before when I graduated from Harvard. The time was 8:59 a.m. I approached the big glass doors, and they opened automatically. I took a deep breath and stepped through.

Inside, I saw a lot of people standing next to the bloodred front desk, which stood in one corner of the spacious lobby, just as the welcome e-mail from my recruiter had instructed me to do. They were all new hires waiting for the first orientation day to start. Just behind the desk hung a huge black SHOW logo. I quickly looked around at the group, which seemed to be made up of about forty people. Most of them appeared to be in their midtwenties. It was our first day, and we were all a part of SHOW now—together. It felt like my first day at Harvard again, full of unknown people and fresh opportunities.

Some of the new hires stood by themselves in the corner of the lobby, like they were afraid of what would happen. Others were chitchatting, while one guy went around hitting on all the women. There were a lot of attractive women in the group—more than I would have imagined in the tech world.

I noticed a guy standing alone by the main door, observing the group from a distance. He had a thick dark beard and was dressed all in black, which distinguished him from the rest. He just stood there and watched, stroking his chin from time to time. Our eyes met and he nodded, so I walked over to introduce myself.

"Hey, I'm Victor. What's up?" I said and reached out my hand.

"Oh, hi. I'm Hank. So many people. Didn't really know what to expect. It's like a whole football team."

"Sure is. The Pro Bowl team. We're a part of it now, man. Aren't you excited?"

"Yeah, I guess. The office is cool at least. Did you see the swimming pool when you were here before?"

"No," I said. "Too bad I hate swimming. Back and forth in a pool filled with chlorinated water, like a goldfish looking for a way out."

I really did hate swimming, but the guy probably thought I was a cynical asshole for being so negative about it. My father always tried to force me to go swimming when I visited him in New York as a kid, but I refused and started to hate it. I usually did the opposite of what he wanted me to do. He thought it would be good for me to swim around like a goldfish. Maybe he was right, maybe not. I had decided he was not.

"But I guess some people will really enjoy the pool," I said in a nice tone, trying to save myself from becoming known as a cynical asshole my first day.

A man with big round glasses began speaking in a loud voice. I didn't see where he came from, and I didn't know who he was. He told us to line up and collect our employee badges from the security personnel sitting behind the front desk. After I'd signed my contract, my recruiter had asked me to send a photo of myself to her. Now I saw that very same photo on a square badge with my name on it. With two lines, the process did not take long, and soon everyone had collected their badges. The guy in glasses told us we had to wear the badges at all times when in the office and that they should always be visible, otherwise security personnel would stop us for an identity check. He added that the badges served as key passes to all doors and gates in the building.

He started heading toward the glass gates blocking the way to a bay with six elevators, and we trailed behind. He said his name was Antonio and that he was the employee onboarding manager. He would give us a tour of the office before we got to the practical things, such as receiving our laptops and meeting our new team of colleagues. He placed his badge on a black sensor, the gate to the elevators opened, and he went through. Everyone followed him.

Because we were a big group, we took the stairs to the first floor. There, Antonio showed us the gym and the swimming pool. Then we tramped up to the fourth floor, which held one of the four restaurants that served breakfast, lunch, and dinner to SHOW employees—all complimentary.

Antonio told us to grab some breakfast and meet by the stairs in forty-five minutes to continue the tour. There was food in excess, including everything I could imagine for breakfast: scrambled eggs, boiled eggs, bacon, sausage, potatoes, fries, fruits, bread, ham, cheese, black beans, pancakes, granola, yogurt, juice, and coffee. A big juice machine squeezed fresh orange juice. I saw a line forming by a counter and went to see what it was for. Once I got closer, I saw that there were four chefs making omelets on demand. The smell made me smile.

I wasn't sure what to eat and in what order, so I took some scrambled eggs and bacon, some bread, and some ham. I saw a table filled with croissants and donuts and grabbed a chocolate donut. Finally, I filled a glass with fresh-squeezed orange juice.

I saw Hank sitting alone at a table by the large windows with a panoramic view of the bay. I walked over and took the free seat opposite him. He had only a bowl of fruit and a croissant to eat. A cup of coffee stood in front of him. He lifted it slowly so he wouldn't spill and took a sip. His lips made a strange movement, and he stuck his tongue out.

"Shit. This coffee is shit. Wise of you to skip it." He wiped his mouth with a napkin.

"Is it? I'm not so demanding when it comes to coffee. I hardly taste the difference," I said.

"I'm sure you'll notice this coffee is shit no matter how bad your taste buds are. At least the melon is really good, juicy."

"I guess I'll have to try the coffee later today and see for myself."
I ate a bite of eggs before asking, "So, what did you do before joining SHOW?"

"Worked with marketing at a fashion start-up here in San Francisco. Ben, one of the two cofounders, cheated on his wife with an intern during a company party. The intern turned out to be the daughter of Ben's wife's yoga teacher in Sausalito. The wife found out; they got divorced. She got the money, and the company went bankrupt. So, here I am." Hank stuck his fork in the last piece of melon.

When we finished our food, we made our way toward the meeting point by the stairs to continue the office tour. As we walked, I watched the employees carrying around mountains of food on their plates. They all seemed to be between twenty-five and thirty-five and wearing their badges visibly as we had just been instructed to do.

I had met a few people when I visited the office during my interviews, but this was the first time I'd seen this many SHOW employees at once. There seemed to be total dress code anarchy. I felt overdressed in my blue shirt. I was glad it was wrinkled.

Antonio was standing in front of the wooden door to the staircase, intensely wiping his glasses with a blue cloth. It was about ten fifty and we all headed up the stairs to the seventh floor. The colors reminded me of the kindergarten I had gone to as a child. The ceiling was red, the floor was green, and the walls were purple. The big windows stretched from floor to ceiling along one entire side of the room and faced South Beach Harbor and the AT&T Park where the Giants play. I stopped for a moment by the window. Once again I had a magnificent view of the world, and the rock star feeling I had had on the plane the day before came back. I had made it to the top. I had made it to the place others in my Harvard class could only dream of.

"Follow me, please," Antonio said.

I turned away from the window and quickly walked after the group. We passed two pool tables and a foosball table. Old arcade games such as Pinball and Pac-Man stood along the purple wall. Employees lay on beanbag chairs and cushions in each corner of the room with laptops on their laps.

Antonio led us to a corner café at one end of the floor. There were soda machines, coffee machines, fruits, and snacks available. Oreo cookies, Snickers, and Skittles were neatly presented as in a store, except these were free.

"Grab whatever you're in the mood for—some snacks, fruit, coffee. Then we'll gather in a conference room and go over some practical details," Antonio said.

I took a bottle of water, a banana, and a Snickers bar. I saw Hank looking at the coffee machine, but it didn't seem to appeal to him, and he ended up with a can of Coke and a pack of Skittles.

Antonio led the way out of the café and along the purple hall. He stopped abruptly and opened a frosted glass door to a room in which white desks and wooden chairs stood in rows facing a wall covered by a whiteboard. The room had white walls and a gray ceiling, and it reminded me of a high school classroom rather than a corporate conference room. "Please have a seat, and I'll present today's agenda. And yes, you will get your laptops today," Antonio said and smiled.

He grabbed a remote lying by the whiteboard and directed it toward a projector hanging from the ceiling. He turned it on, and the day's agenda appeared on the whiteboard in front of us.

According to the agenda, we would get our laptops, learn about data security, have some lunch with our respective managers, and then meet with a benefits manager as a group. Then there would be a few free hours before a welcome dinner at seven o'clock. SHOW had reserved an entire restaurant close to the office.

"Pretty clear, right?" said Antonio. "If there are no other questions, let me give you something to think about. Most people believe that if it ain't broke, don't fix it. Engineers believe that if it ain't broke, it doesn't have enough features yet." He burst into laughter.

I smiled, and a few people laughed loudly at the joke, but most were quiet. Maybe they were afraid to laugh, thinking it was a test to see which of us would laugh at engineers.

Just as Antonio's laughter started to fade away, I heard a knock on the door and saw some shapes behind the glass. Antonio opened the door, and two guys with glasses and black SHOW T-shirts walked in. They had a little trolley piled with new laptops.

Antonio told us to line up and collect our laptops. I received mine and signed a form acknowledging I'd collected the corporate computer and then returned to my seat to set up my password. I heard another knock on the door and looked at my watch. It was 11:57 a.m.

A guy with a ponytail and a ring in his nose walked into the room with a Lenovo laptop under his right arm. He was skinny and pale and had the numbers 001100 tattooed on his left elbow. I used his tattoo as inspiration for my password, combining it with my initials, V. J. for Victor Janoski. The cursor blinked in the empty password box. I typed V001100J and hit "Enter" on the keyboard.

Antonio introduced the man with the ponytail. His name was Jeff, and he talked to us about the importance of data security, how sensitive the information SHOW stored was, and why such information couldn't be leaked to the public. Jeff mainly discussed the information stored about SHOW's clients, specifically the companies that used the online advertising products. He stressed that leaking corporate information or violating any of the security policies would lead to immediate termination from SHOW.

Once Jeff was done talking about the security protocols, he told us to access a digital form on our laptops and mark the checkbox that stated we'd heard and understood the information he'd just provided. Then he put his Lenovo under his arm and walked out without another word.

"Well, now you've seen a real SHOW engineer," Antonio said once Jeff was gone.

A woman put her hand up and made eye contact with Antonio. He nodded toward her with a smile.

"Antonio, has anyone ever leaked anything secret and been fired?"

"What's your name?" he answered.

"Nicky."

"Nice to meet you, Nicky. No, nobody has been fired as far as I know. But that doesn't mean you shouldn't follow the policies." He smiled and then turned back to the group. "Okay, everyone, nice job. It's time for lunch. Your managers will come to this room and pick you up. I'll see you back here at two." With that, Antonio left the room.

My manager's name was Louise. She'd been the last person of the four I'd interviewed with when I'd visited SHOW the first time. During my interview, she'd smiled constantly while asking me questions. It had made me slightly uneasy because I'd thought she was only smiling to make me feel comfortable with my answers even though she hated them. It seemed this hadn't been the case because I was offered the job one month later with an October start date. Louise looked to be in her midthirties and was skinny with blond hair. She'd moved from San Diego up to San Francisco for the job four years earlier.

I saw her scurrying into the room with her MacBook under her arm. Her hair was braided, and she wore bootcut jeans and a white top. She noticed me and smiled. I smiled back, closed my laptop, and walked over to her.

"Hey, Vic. So nice to see you again. Welcome!"

"Hi, Louise. Thanks. I'm happy to finally be here. Really excited."

"Great to hear! I hope you're hungry. I'll just need to find your new teammates, Hank and Gabe. Then we'll have lunch together."

Louise gathered them, and I introduced myself to Gabe and said hi to Hank again. We followed Louise down the stairs to the cafeteria on the fourth floor. She took a seat at a table next to the floor-to-ceiling windows facing the bay. She was only having yogurt and told us to go and grab food while she held the seats.

I couldn't believe how many types of food were available. There was a salad bar, a stand with vegetarian food, and two additional stations with other dishes. There were lines of people everywhere, so I decided to randomly pick one. I ended up with a braised leg of lamb with gravy and mashed potatoes on one plate and asparagus, corn on the cob, and Caesar salad on a second.

I made my way back to the table with my two plates and sat opposite Gabe, with the window on my right. Louise sat on my left, while Hank sat across from her. Gabe's dark hair was thick and wavy. He was quite tall and in good shape—but not like he went to the gym five days a week and lifted heavy weights until he was so muscled he could barely move. No, he was more like a triathlete. One might say he was in perfect shape. His round black glasses made him seem intelligent, although I didn't know if he was or not. Time would tell.

I noticed Hank was bent over a big bowl of salad with cooked salmon on top, while Gabe was digging into a leg of lamb. Louise was drinking low-fat yogurt. I thought she might be on a diet, but I couldn't figure out why considering how skinny she was. I didn't ask.

Louise said she was happy to see us and that the team was excited we had joined the company. She spent about thirty minutes telling us how amazing it was to work at SHOW, including the career possibilities, the ability to make an impact, the people, the benefits, and—last but not least—the crazy parties. We listened carefully while chewing our food.

Hank constantly wiped his mouth with a napkin and stroked his beard, making sure no salad leaves or salmon pieces got stuck in it. Through his glasses, Gabe seemed to be trying to constantly maintain eye contact with Louise, while nodding politely and responding with comments like "Oh wow, that's amazing" to everything she said.

Personally, I was just enjoying the moment. As I listened to Louise, I watched the boats sailing in the bay. I wondered where they were headed. Who were the people in them, and how had they ended up together on those ships? I wondered where SHOW would take me. Wherever it was, I looked forward to starting the journey.

Louise suddenly stopped talking and said she had to run to a meeting but that we would catch up later that week. She stood up, wished us good luck with the rest of the introduction week, and sprinted toward the elevator with her laptop under her arm.

We took the stairs back up to the seventh-floor conference room and took a seat to listen to the presentation by the benefits manager. The door opened, and a woman holding an open MacBook to her chest came into the room. She was so overweight she had trouble moving. Her body shifted from side to side like a duck as she headed to the front of the room. She wore a blue blouse, white jeans, and a red scarf around her neck, which she kept touching as if to make sure it didn't fall off.

She introduced herself as Monica from the corporate benefits team and said that if we had any questions about the benefits we could e-mail her department—seven days a week, day and night—and always get a reply within four hours.

Monica wirelessly connected her computer to the projector, and Antonio used the remote to switch it on. A long list of corporate benefits showed up on the wall, such as on-site massage; three meals per day; on-site dentist and doctor; and complimentary drinks, fruit, and snacks.

She explained each benefit one by one. By the middle, I was so overwhelmed I stopped listening. I didn't know where to start and what to take advantage of first. They had really covered everything. Once Monica was done with the main list, she launched into a discussion about benefits for employees with children. I glanced at Hank, who sat on my right. He seemed bored and was scrolling through pictures of sneakers on Amazon on his iPhone. He looked up and noticed I was staring at his phone screen. He leaned over to me.

"You drink whiskey?"

"Sometimes," I said.

"Let's go for one before the dinner."

"Okay, if we have time."

"Yeah, yeah, we will. I know a place."

My watch said 4:08 p.m. The benefits presentation had already exceeded its scheduled time, and it was still going. People had questions about a lot of things, such as if we were allowed to take food and snacks home or even the towels from the gym. One person asked if we could bring friends and family to the swimming pool and another if we were allowed to expense private tennis classes to the company.

At four thirty, Monica stopped the questions and said we could e-mail the benefits department if we had any further musings. She picked up her MacBook, wished us a pleasant welcoming dinner, and pushed her way out the door. Antonio also wished us a nice dinner and followed her out.

Hank and I quickly put our laptops under our arms and bounded down the stairs. Once on the ground floor, we put the computers in Hank's black backpack and hurried through the automatic gates, past the reception desk, and out onto the street and into the rain.

"Classic fucking October," Hank said.

"What do you mean?"

"The weather. Let's go."

We took a left and headed southwest on Townsend Street. The bay was behind us, and a light drizzle blew straight into our faces. As we took a right onto Fourth Street and continued north toward Market Street, the drizzle slowly started to become light rain and began hitting us from the side. When we got to Bryant Street, Hank stopped and opened a green door in a light-green building on the corner.

"This is it," Hank said and walked inside.

The three-story building had bay windows jutting out all the way around. I noticed the brown sign above the door: it said "The Utah Inn" in white letters. As I stood and looked at the building, the rain started to get heavier. The bartender yelled to close the door, so I went inside and did as he asked.

The room was narrow. On the right side, a row of windows stretched from the entrance to the end of the room. On the left, Hank was already sitting on one of the stools at the long mahogany bar, which ran the length of the entire place. Round white glass lamps hung from the ceiling above, exuding a dim light. The dark wooden floor creaked as I crossed the restaurant and took a seat next to Hank.

The bartender, who wore a black T-shirt and an orange San Francisco Giants cap, poured Jameson whiskey into two glasses, each filled with ice and topped with a slice of lime. Then he added ginger ale.

"Enjoy, guys," he said.

"Thanks," Hank said. He grabbed his drink and turned to me. "Cheers and welcome to whiskey ginger." He took a big sip.

"Cheers."

"Fuck, it's good!" Hank licked his lips.

"This is a cool place. You come here often?" I asked.

"Yeah. Nice crowd. No fucking suits. I come here when I want to relax, couple times a month. Gangsters, writers, and even Marilyn Monroe used to come here for drinks. It's a classic bar, more than a hundred years old. It was here even before Prohibition."

"Really? I bet some crazy things have happened here over the years."

"Yeah, I heard the owner in the fifties didn't like neckties and cut them off with scissors if someone came in wearing one. I like that. Fucking suits."

"I'm not a fan either," I said. "My dad used to force me to wear a shirt and tie at Christmas. It was too tight around my neck. I didn't like being forced to do shit like that."

Hank laughed. "So did mine when I was a kid. My family moved around a lot. My mom has been working as a diplomat at the US embassy in France since before I left for college, and before that she was at the embassy in Sweden for two years. Every time we had some fucking diplomat guests for dinner at home, I had to wear a shirt and tie."

"So you lived in France and Sweden?"

"Yeah, but I was born in Seattle. Moved to DC when I was ten, when my mom got a gig at the US Department of State. Dad stayed in Seattle. He worked at the Starbucks headquarters—a suit selling shitty coffee. I hated the smell of those beans he used to bring home from the office."

"So you're not the kind of guy who takes pictures of your Starbucks cup and posts them online?" I grinned.

"Fuck no. I hate those people. The coffee is horrible, and the shops are too."

"I agree, man. Standardized with no soul. Just a brand. The McDonald's of coffee."

Hank took a drink of his whiskey. "We left DC for Sweden when I was fifteen. They had no Starbucks there then, and I loved not having to see that green fucking sign all day. I remember the Swedes mainly drank their coffee black. Not all the shitty Starbucks triple mocha diet latte with extra cream."

"Fucking retarded," I said. "Welcome to LA coffee life. My older sister, Emma, fits that profile. She and her friends drink grande diet lattes, or light or whatever it is, with extra cream. Why the fuck do you order a diet if you're gonna add cream? Then they take a picture of the cup and post it on Instagram. If Starbucks paid them every time, they'd be rich."

"That's fucked. I need another." Hank waved to the bartender, who was watching the Giants game on a small TV hanging on the wall behind the bar. The Giants were losing six to fourteen against the Nationals at Nationals Park in DC.

"They're so bad this year. I could do better myself. Two more?" the bartender said.

"Yeah, fill 'er up," Hank said.

I took a sip of my fresh drink and polished my teeth with my tongue to clean the sugar from the ginger ale off them.

"So, you're from Hollywood town?" Hank asked.

"Yep, the city of broken dreams. Born and raised."

"Cool. I like Venice. All the crazy people and the smell of weed floating in the air."

"It has its charm. I like the crazy people too. They chase their dreams until they die. They don't give a fuck. I kind of admire them for not giving up their artistic ambitions."

"And what's your dream? Hollywood star?" Hank grinned.

"Ha ha. That's my sister's dream. She's been struggling for ten years now, not wanting to accept she has no acting talent except being a drama queen, which she's good at in a natural way. No acting required."

"I thought everyone wanted to become a fucking celebrity down there. Then they end up under a bridge once their dream fails."

"Well, you're not totally wrong," I said. "I had a dream of being a screenwriter before going to Harvard. My dad insisted I get an education and a real job instead. He didn't want me to end up at the Venice Boardwalk selling crappy poems written on stolen McDonald's napkins."

"So I guess he's proud of you getting a job at SHOW straight out of school."

"Nah, he's old and says online advertising isn't real work: it lacks creativity, artistic skill, and talent. He lives in New York and worked as an art director at a big advertising firm before he retired a while back. Says ads are an art form and the ugly digital banners are a disgrace to the entire advertising industry. Anyway, how about you? What's your big dream?"

Hank sat quietly on the bar stool and shrugged his shoulders like an Italian gangster boss forced to decide if a disloyal cousin should be shot or not. "I need to take a leak." He got up from the bar stool. "Order another round."

The bartender was standing at the end of the bar chatting with a middle-aged lady. I waved to him and pointed at our empty glasses. He gave me the thumbs-up and turned back to the woman.

I looked at my watch: 6:27 p.m. The dinner would start at seven. The new drinks arrived just as Hank came back from the bathroom. I told him we needed to hurry, but he didn't seem to care and told me to relax. We finished our drinks in less than ten minutes, and Hank left seventy-five dollars under one of the glasses. He put his backpack on and started toward the door. I saw that the Giants were down by eleven when we passed the TV on our way out.

* * *

It had stopped drizzling, and we slogged down Fourth Street to Townsend Street, then took a left off Townsend onto Lusk Street and saw the restaurant. We went straight inside and were greeted by the host, who asked us if we were there for the SHOW dinner. I said yes, and we followed him downstairs to the private dining area. People were already sitting at two long tables pushed close to each other. I saw a free spot at the end of one of the tables and walked over to take a seat opposite Gabe. I said hi to him before I introduced myself to the woman in a white top on his left. It was Nicky, the one who'd asked about leaking corporate secrets. Her brown eyes almost drowned in her face as she smiled at me while stroking her black braided hair with both hands. A cute blond sat on my right. I introduced myself, and she said her name was Chloe.

The table was covered with a white tablecloth and bottles of San Pellegrino water stood in the middle. We each had a menu in front of us listing three different starters, mains, and desserts to choose from.

A waiter in a white shirt appeared by our side of the table. "Any drinks to start with? Beer? Wine?"

"Gabe, do you drink whiskey?" I asked.

"I do from time to time. I didn't plan to drink liquor tonight, though."

"Ah, come on. See it as a celebration drink."

He appeared a bit troubled and hesitated. "Well, okay, let's go for one. If my girlfriend gets mad at me for stinking like a distillery, I'm gonna blame you." He smiled.

"One old-fashioned each, please," I told the waiter.

Without a word, the waiter turned to the women to take their orders.

"So you live together? You and the girlfriend," I said to Gabe.

"Yeah, we've been together for three years. Met at Yale. We moved into an apartment up in Noe Valley last week."

"Congratulations, sounds nice."

"Thanks. Yeah, it's a nice area. Will be interesting trying to live together as well. Where do you live?" Gabe said.

"At the Hyatt up by Market Street for the moment. I only arrived from LA yesterday, so I'll have to look for a place this week. Anyway, how'd you end up at SHOW?"

Gabe explained that he had an MBA from Yale and had grown up in Manhattan. He was a bicycling enthusiast, and as a teenager he'd shown promising talent and had been a member of the junior national cycling team. His big dream had been to make it to the Olympics, but life had taken him elsewhere.

"Man, why'd you quit if you were that good?" I asked.

"Well, honestly, I didn't wanna quit," he said.

"So? And? Elaborate?"

"You see, my father is a Wall Street man, a broker—highly successful one actually. He didn't consider my cycling career serious and wanted me to become a Wall Street broker like him."

The waiter brought the drinks from the bar. "Old-fashioned for you, sir, and old-fashioned for you, sir." He put the drinks on the table and left.

"All my father's friends are Wall Street brokers. They all want their kids to go the same way. They feel ashamed of their kids if they don't go into business. So he pushed me to go to Yale, same school he went to."

"Sad to hear that . . . or from a selfish perspective glad, since we're drinking whiskey together now." I motioned with my glass. "So Yale, hard to get accepted to I heard—congrats."

"I suppose. I had good grades, not the best, though. But since Dad was a Yale alumnus, he had some connections that helped me in. After all, it was him pushing me to go there, so he had to fix it," Gabe said.

"So, business was your second dream after the cycling, I guess?" I said.

"No, no, but I guess that's what you're supposed to do. And Dad, of course, wanted me to deal with business and stocks. I never wanted to work on Wall Street like him and a lot of my classmates. I think tech is the future: it's the new Wall Street. Without the greed and bad things." He took a sip of his drink.

"Yeah, I heard there's a lot of greed there. I had a childhood friend working on Wall Street once—John. He said it was a crazy lifestyle and hard to get out of once you'd started, even though he wasn't really a fan."

"Yes, once a Wall Street man, always a Wall Street man."

"Anyway, now you're here," I said. "You never know where you'll end up in life. But it's never too late. One day you'll be a cycling champion and win an Olympic gold medal—on PlayStation, that is." I lifted my glass to cheers.

We laughed and sipped our drinks. It was a magnificent old-fashioned, close to perfect. Not too sweet, the ice not too crushed, and no weird twists such as cherries on top to ruin it.

We browsed our menus and were ready to order when the waiter came just two minutes later. We selected an assortment, and I ended up with beef carpaccio, smoked duck breast, and a salted-caramel swirl brownie.

It was hot inside the restaurant. The air-conditioning wasn't up to keeping a group of forty people cool in such a small space. Someone on the other side of my table proposed we stand up one by one and introduce ourselves briefly. Most seemed to think it was a good idea, and so the introductions started.

It quickly became clear we were all graduates from top-tier universities who chased success and glory. We had a variety of skill sets. There was a helicopter pilot, a woman who spoke six languages fluently, and a guy with an online store that sold swords. They all had something special, something extraordinary. I loved it. I even admired the person who collected stamps and had over ten thousand of them from all around the globe. Nicky said she was a former skydiving instructor, while Chloe was a runner and had participated in sixteen marathons.

I had been writing a bit, mainly short stories and articles. The year before I'd had two op-ed pieces published in the *Boston Globe*. My skills paled in comparison to those of the others, but I was still proud.

The appetizers arrived quickly. My beef carpaccio was perfect and melted in my mouth. As soon as I finished it, my duck was served. It was well-balanced and smoked to perfection.

"So, Vic, what brought you to SHOW?" Gabe said.

"Well, honestly, I didn't have plans to work at SHOW or in tech specifically. I studied business at Harvard but never wanted to end up in a big corporation.

"You got headhunted to SHOW?" Gabe asked.

"Nah, a friend of mine from Harvard thought this place would suit me. So, hell, why not? I thought and applied. I'm really happy to be here, though. It's gonna be awesome."

The waiter came in with the dessert. I cut a bite of the brownie with my fork and put it in my mouth. It melted, just as the carpaccio had. I loved it when food was so good you wanted to let it melt in your mouth forever.

I tried to make conversation with Chloe, but she seemed very uptight, almost rude. She was talking to Nicky and the women to her right, and they didn't seem to want to let Gabe or me in on their conversation. Every now and then, Chloe dragged her blond hair behind her ear with her left hand, and I'd look at her. Her ears were cute. I wondered if she found my staring unpleasant. After several attempts to make conversation, I stopped trying and ignored her.

After dessert, Gabe, Hank, and I decided to leave the dinner party and head to a bar on Second Street that Hank liked. We said good-bye to our new colleagues, walked up the stairs, and out to the street. We encountered light headwinds on Second Street. The breeze was nice and cooling, which we highly appreciated after the stuffiness of the restaurant.

We took a seat at the bar and ordered a round of Jack and a bowl of chili peanuts. The place had a dark wooden interior and was half empty and dimly lit. Whiskey barrels served as tables. Guns N' Roses was playing from the speakers, and the bartender was doing an air guitar solo, pretending to be Slash.

"So guys, what do you think after the first day? It's pretty sweet, right?" asked Hank while chewing the peanuts like a squirrel.

"Yes, it's interesting," Gabe said.

"Yeah, it's cool so far," I agreed. "Nice people. I'm excited to start working when the intro week is done."

Two women sitting at the other end of the bar drinking martinis had been staring at us since the moment we sat down. They were attractive and appeared to be in their midtwenties. One had dark hair and wore a low-cut red dress. She had a gold watch on her right hand that she constantly played with, like she was checking that it was still there. Either it was expensive or it had sentimental value to her.

The other woman had light-brown hair. She wore a black skirt, black Louboutin heels, and a white silk shirt that was not fully buttoned. I could see her black bra when she leaned forward and laughed. She had two silver bracelets on her left wrist and dark-red nail polish that looked even darker in contrast with her white shirt.

I imagined they were models out for drinks and discussing men, waiting for some pretty boys to buy them martinis and charm them like James Bond. I wished I could pull that off, but I didn't dare try. I couldn't handle the risk of rejection. Not trying was the safest bet. It completely eliminated all risk of rejection—a risk I'd been highly aware of since my girlfriend, Amanda, had suddenly left me on our one-year anniversary one year before.

Out of nowhere, the bartender put three glasses of whiskey in front of us.

"From the two ladies at the bar." He smiled.

Gabe got a bit nervous and didn't know how to react. I assumed he felt guilty because he had a girlfriend waiting at home. Here he was, living like a rock star, drinking whiskey on a Monday evening with sexy models sending him drinks.

We all looked at the women, and once we made eye contact, nodded our heads, smiled, and held our glasses up to cheers them. As soon as we took our first sips, the women left their chairs and sauntered toward us. You could imagine how their bodies moved in sync just by listening to the sound of their heels hitting the wooden floor. The bartender seemed surprised by what was happening.

"Hey, guys, how are the drinks?" the woman with the black skirt asked with a little smile.

"Fucking delicious," Hank said, playing it cool. "How's your night, ladies?" He took some peanuts from the bowl and threw them in his mouth.

"It's wonderful. Good drinks, nice company," said the one with the red dress, still playing with her watch.

"And good-looking guys," added the other.

Gabe was sitting quietly while I planned my winning line to charm them. Hank didn't seem to care about them.

"I like your shoes," I said to the one with the Louboutins, for lack of anything better to say.

"You like my shoes?" She laughed while her white shirt slipped down on her left shoulder so that I could see a black bra strap.

"Yeah, I do. So do you work around here in one of the tech firms?" I asked.

"No, we're fashion designers," replied the woman in the red dress. She turned to Hank. "Anyhow, we just adore your clothes and think you look so chic. We'd like to take some pictures with you, if that's okay?"

"Yeah, sure. Why not? Let's do it," Hank answered.

They took some pictures of him and with him using their phones, asked about his clothes, gave him their business cards, and left. Hank glanced at the cards, muttered something, and threw them on the bar. I'd never seen a guy that uninterested in beautiful women. I appreciated it in a way. It could mean only two things: Hank was gay, or he had enough integrity to not think with his dick. A third scenario might be that he was too drunk to understand what was going on, but since he was still sitting on the bar stool, I excluded that possibility.

"Hey, bud, did you see that they were smoking hot? They gave you their business cards, and you just threw them away," I said.

"Yeah, I know, but they weren't my type. Too shallow and seemed dumb as fuck."

"Agreed," Gabe said. "So Hank, your clothes. You like fashion, I guess. The ladies seemed impressed."

"Yeah, I even design some clothes myself. I'll tell you about it another day." Hank stroked his thick beard.

I went to the bathroom, and when I came back, Hank was gone. Gabe said he'd chugged his drink, said bye, and left. And so did we.

3

When I woke up at my hotel the next morning, I could hear the rain smashing against the window like a group of angry woodpeckers pecking at a tree. My eyes were still closed, and I imagined the massive storm going on outside. My head felt like a heavy bowling ball hitting all the pins at once.

Fuck you, whiskey: you and your delicious taste; you and your beautiful color. Fuck you. Afraid of the pain, I didn't dare open my eyes—not yet. I decided to fall back asleep.

When I woke up again, I could feel the heat on my left cheek, feel the light through my eyelids. I slowly opened my left eye. The sun was shining straight on me through the window. I'd forgotten to close the blinds when I got back to the room the night before. I closed my eye. It felt like I had the sand of the entire Sahara in my mouth, and I craved water like a dying plant abandoned by its owner. I grabbed my silver watch from the nightstand and saw it was 9:53 a.m.

After a couple of seconds, I realized that I was late for my second day of work. I jumped out of bed, went to the bathroom, put my mouth under the tap like an animal, and drank until I almost choked. I splashed some cold water in my face and sprayed on some Armani cologne to get rid of the dirty bar scent.

My head was still a disaster. I took two aspirins, put on my pants, socks, and shoes, and grabbed a shirt from my suitcase before running to the elevator. It was out of order so I took the staircase down to the lobby and ran out on the street to hail a cab. The cabdriver looked at me like I was a crazy person when I jumped into his car shirtless. I put my shirt on and told him to stop fucking staring and start driving to SHOW.

"Eight to nineteen," the driver said.

"Sorry?"

"Giants, they lost, eight to nineteen. Horrible game."

"Sure, terrible."

We arrived outside the office at 10:11 a.m., and five minutes later I was in the conference room on the seventh floor. My NewSHOWers group, as SHOW called the cohorts of new employees, was listening to a guy wearing glasses and a black T-shirt with a pink rhino on it. I took a seat in the back row, like the cool kids in school always did—the kids that didn't give a fuck and were out smoking cigarettes for most of class.

I bet they're not as successful as I am now, idiots. They should have listened to their teachers. Now I had a swimming pool at the office, and they didn't.

My eyes wandered around the room, and I didn't really pay attention to the guy talking. There was still a rock concert going in my head; it felt like the drummer of Metallica was using my brain as his drum set.

A lot of familiar faces from the previous night were in the room. Some seemed like they had just gotten out from the bar, others like they'd slept in a ditch. Several people I remembered were not even there, though, so I guess I was not so bad for being late after all. I treated myself to the Snickers bar I'd grabbed in the lobby when I'd walked into the office. My conscience was clean.

The day continued in the same way as the previous one, with presentations and practical information. When it was over at five o'clock, I wandered back to my hotel.

By the time I got back to my room, my hangover had vanished. I found a small bottle of Jameson in the minibar and poured a glass. *I fucking love you, whiskey. You and your beautiful color, you and your delicious taste—how you make me feel. I fucking love you. I even love the hangover. It gives me the feeling that things can only get better from now on.*

I fell asleep on the bed with my clothes on to the tune of Billy Joel's "Piano Man."

4

For the entire first week at the office, each day was similar to the last: we were taught the company culture, had some product training in SHOW's advertising solutions, and played a lot of video games. After work, we usually went out to party. A lot of the conversations were a competition—a cockfight—of who had done the coolest things and who was the smartest and the best.

On Friday, another day of advertising solutions trainings had come to an end. At Nicky's suggestion, the entire group decided to go out for dinner and drinks at a Thai restaurant near the office.

Friday also meant that it was time for FridayShow, SHOW's weekly happy hour. Every Friday at five o'clock, the cafeteria on the twenty-first floor—the top floor—transformed into an open bar. This would be our first FridayShow as new hires, and we planned to stop by for drinks before our dinner at six thirty.

In the cafeteria, a band made up of three guys and a woman played covers on a small stage temporarily assembled at one end of the room. Old classics like "Summer of '69" by Bryan Adams and "You're the Voice" by John Farnham came out of the speakers.

Hank was disappointed to realize they didn't serve liquor at FridayShow and settled for a Budweiser, which he didn't like but said did the job better than water. We stayed for only an hour before leaving the office and heading to the restaurant together.

When we walked into the restaurant, a lady started shouting something in Thai to the waiters, and they all disappeared like ninjas into the kitchen, leaving us alone with her.

"Follow me!" she yelled and began to weave through the restaurant.

"Okay, lady," Nicky said.

We zigzagged behind her between the tables and other guests. It was noisy, with people talking, laughing, and greedily slurping noodles into their mouths. The smell of fried spring rolls and coconut milk hovered over the room. There were paintings of Buddha on the wall, and orchids in round white vases stood on each table. The orchids made me think of my father, who used to take me to the New York Botanical Garden every summer when I visited him.

We were seated at a long table covered in a yellow tablecloth. It was time again: time for the cockfights; time to see who had the best stories. I drank Thai whiskey, ate Pad Thai, and drank more Thai whiskey. After dinner, we ordered several taxis and went to a club by Union Square. Some people danced, some smoked weed, some did coke. Nicky made out with a man on the dance floor, and one guy vomited into an ice bucket on a table.

It was a show. The young elite were on fire. My first week of work had come to an end. I don't remember how I got back to the Hyatt to drown in the mattress that night.

5

"The refrigerator is brand-new, as you can see. The stove's not too shabby either, and the microwave is just about six months old."

Bob was giving me a morning tour of a 350-square-foot studio apartment in a three-story building on Twenty-Fourth Street in the Mission District, between Valencia Street and Guerrero Street. He was around sixty years old and had hair as white as Oreo cookie filling. His small glasses made him look like an old Harry Potter who'd had more whiskey than he could handle.

My head pounded as I listened to Bob explaining the details. I didn't care that the microwave was only six months old. I just wanted to lie down on the hardwood floor and pass out.

"There's a laundromat in the building next door and a Whole Foods store close by. What do you do for a living?" Bob said.

"I work in tech."

"Oh, you're one of those. Then this is perfect for you."

"How much is the rent?" I asked.

"It's twenty-three hundred fine American dollars a month, plus utilities. Sign a one-year lease, and you're ready to move in."

I was making $82,000 a year. I didn't need a roommate anymore. "Where do I sign?"

Bob said he'd arrange the paperwork while I went for a coffee. I could come back in an hour to sign the lease and collect the keys. I went down the stairs and out onto the street. From there, I looked up at the building, which I hadn't had the chance to examine closely before.

It was light yellow with dark-green trim. Each floor was distinguished by a thick line of green. My new apartment was on the top floor. From the sidewalk, six steps led up to a double door with light-green stained glass windows. The gold doorknob reflected the sunlight straight into my eyes, so I turned away and set off to a nearby café. There I ordered a bottle of water and an espresso and wondered if this was the life I would live from now on—constant drinking and partying. I wasn't used to it.

My years at Harvard had been tough. I'd had to work hard to get the top grades I needed to get a job at a good company right after graduation. I'd wanted to prove to my father that I was good enough, that I could make it. I'd wanted to make him proud of me, which was not easy. He was a demanding man: nothing was ever good enough. The fact that he was paying for my education had made me want to succeed even more.

I didn't drink or party much at all during my years at school, although my best friend and roommate, Daniel, did. Daniel was from Sugar Land, Texas, and unlike me, his focus at Harvard was less on studies and more on partying and chasing girls. Every now and then I'd join him at a party. At one of them I met a language and literacy student named Amanda. Our first date was to a pancake place in Boston. She became my first love and girlfriend.

Despite Daniel's lack of focus at Harvard, he'd also been hired by SHOW and was scheduled to start three weeks after me. His persona and entrepreneurial spirit had compensated for his bad grades, although it had taken three extra interviews and an additional review of his application before the offer came. It had been Daniel who convinced me to apply to SHOW. He'd been talking about it for years, dreaming of working there, and he was convinced SHOW was the best company in the world. I hadn't had any other plans, so two weeks before graduation we'd both applied for account manager positions.

I took a sip of the espresso. The sour taste on my tongue gave me a kick. I opened the water bottle and drank almost half in one go. It felt like a waterfall in my chest. So far my job didn't feel like a real job, though I suspected once I actually started it would be demanding, with long hours. Since being offered the position, I'd been afraid that I couldn't manage it, that I wasn't good enough. I was afraid of the pressure, as well as of being sucked into the chase for artificial success created by society.

The number of drinks and drugs I'd seen being consumed with ease by colleagues made me think of my childhood friend John. He'd been working on Wall Street when he'd OD'd in his apartment in New York and passed away.

My phone rang. It was Bob. He was already done with the paperwork, and I could come and sign right away. He was in a hurry to get to the horse track. His favorite horse, Stay Thirsty, was running today, and he couldn't miss it.

I walked out of the café and back to see Bob. As I climbed up the stairs to the apartment, my head pounded even harder. Once inside, Bob handed me a pen and showed me the contract papers lined up by the kitchen sink. I signed them, and Bob gave me a key chain with two sets of keys. I wished Bob all the best at the horse track and closed the door behind him. I had to go back to the Hyatt to check out and get my suitcases, but first I decided to lie down on the hardwood floor and close my eyes for a while. My new life now had a new home.

6

After two weeks of training, I began to work on my own and became fully responsible for the companies in my advertising portfolio. The sales department I worked in consisted of more than a thousand people. We were a big firm, and we were only getting bigger. My team consisted of twenty people, Hank and Gabe among them. We were the fresh account managers for the team that handled entertainment industry clients, such as movie studios, record labels, and movie theater chains.

Our boss, Louise, talked very fast and was highly energetic, constantly moving. She normally didn't even walk; instead she always ran. She usually wore her blond hair in a severe ponytail with a red hair band, and she wore bootcut jeans and a T-shirt every day. Some days her shirt had a cartoon character like Donald Duck on it.

It was Tuesday morning, and I was about to have a meeting with Louise to discuss my time at SHOW so far and what my expectations of the job and long-term goals at the company were. I was sitting at my desk reading a sexual harassment company policy that I had to sign when a reminder popped up on my screen. It was ten thirty. Time for the meeting with Louise.

Her desk was just three rows away from mine in the open-layout office. She was staring at her screen and hitting the keys on the keyboard like they were made of stone. Three cans of Diet Coke stood to the right of the screen, and empty Oreo cookie packages lay scattered just above her keyboard.

"Oh, just give me one minute, Vic—have to finish up this e-mail." She looked at the keyboard, wondering which key to hit next.

"No worries. I'll grab a coffee and wait for you in the meeting room named Growth."

In the cafeteria, I bumped into Hank standing by the coffee machine with a brown paper bag in his hand, smelling it deeply. He wore an oversized black shirt and black pants, along with white high-tops. Hank was a coffee expert; it was one of his things. He had even lived in Colombia for a year to study the art of coffee, making his living working on a coffee bean farm. His passion for good quality coffee was born while he lived in Paris and noticed there were places other than Starbucks. He was extremely picky about what he drank and refused to drink the shit they served at the office. He brought his own beans to work. Apparently there were other java freaks around, and they'd formed a club that hosted special gatherings where they drank their fancy brews. Others weren't allowed to join them or to touch their stuff.

Since Hank stood there with the special beans in hand, I took the opportunity to ask if he could make me some. He said he would make an exception for me and started to work his magic. After a couple of minutes, he served me. The beverage smelled good and tasted like coffee. I told him it was the best I had ever drunk in my life. Hank went out for a smoke with his own precious cup, and I went to the meeting room to wait for my boss.

I waited fifteen minutes. Louise didn't show. Maybe she had gotten lost on the way, or found the Oreo cookie storage. I finally went back to my desk and found her there, babbling to a colleague of mine about some sales numbers. It sounded like she was complaining.

"Oh, there you are, Vic. I was just telling Eric here that the sales numbers for this week don't look pretty. Sorry I missed our meeting, but we're in trouble, and I have to figure something out." "I understand. Let me know if I can do anything," I said. "If you're not on the phone, you're not selling. Try making some sales calls. I have to polish these numbers now and make them better before reporting to upper management." She turned and hurried away.

I sat down at my desk and signed the sexual harassment policy. I didn't plan to harass anyone, so I didn't read it all. I wondered what Louise meant by "polishing the numbers." I guessed I would learn how things were done.

While browsing my client portfolio, I decided to call a Hollywood studio to discuss the online advertising for their newest movies to boost ticket sales and improve my sales numbers. My trick to make them spend more was to ask them if they wanted to spend less money while getting better results with their ads. The more I did it, the better I got at it. I liked that I had more power and knowledge in the advertising field than my clients.

I'd always considered knowledge to be the most powerful tool you could have. It's one of the things nobody can take away from you—knowledge and memories. They are like stories written in indelible ink.

7

I arrived early at work one morning and was making my way across the corporate parking lot. It was already filled with cars at eight o'clock. The air was foggy, and I could barely see where I was going. Workers were running with take-out coffee cups in hand, weaving through the maze of parked cars—the first mental challenge of the day.

Suddenly I heard honking behind me. I turned around and saw a massive Jeep coming out of the mist. Unlike a normal Wrangler, this one was huge. It was black and orange and had gigantic black wheels, almost like a monster truck. An orange grid protected big headlights on the roof, and a solid orange jack was mounted on the front hood.

I was wondering why the idiot was honking at me when the vehicle stopped right next to me. The tinted window on the driver's side slowly slid down, and I saw a big smile. It was my friend from Harvard, Daniel. He was starting at SHOW that week.

"Heeey, man! What's up?" Daniel jumped down to hug me.

"Hey, Daniel! You crazy fuck. What's that?"

He laughed. I asked him again, and he laughed again. Then he looked at me with a sly smile. "Ah, it's a Jeep. I did a good deal on a new side project. I'll tell you later. I have to run now. I'm already late on my first day."

He crawled back up into the car—which was blocking half the lane—and drove away, leaving only a rumbling sound in his wake. Daniel was the most positive person I knew. He usually acted like nothing could stop him and didn't back off from anything. His persistence was one of his big strengths, as well as a weakness. Things didn't always turn out the way he wanted, and he had a hard time letting go. Sometimes he became like a wild greyhound chasing an adrenaline-fueled rabbit.

He was obsessed with orange—the color, not the fruit, although he liked the fruit as well. Besides the orange-and-black monster of a car, he had an orange bike, an orange watch, and an orange MacBook. He claimed orange was the color of success, the color for winners.

His other obsession was Apple and their products. He was one of the people you saw on the news lining up for days and sleeping outside the store when new products like the Apple Watch were released. Although I couldn't understand that passion, I was somehow jealous of it. It was completely stupid, but at the same time I was envious of devotion that strong, the urge to want something so much you'd sleep on a sidewalk for it. Why would you want to wait in line for days to buy a tech product? You could just buy it a couple of days later with no line. It would be the same product—and probably better since they had had time to test it on the morons who got it first. Daniel said that it was a part of the world's evolution, and he wanted to be first, like Neil Armstrong on the moon.

8

Each morning after breakfast at the office restaurant, we would walk over to the cafeteria on our floor for coffee. Our teammate Eric made it for us. He claimed to be an expert at it, which he wasn't, but he was good enough. Hank, the real coffee expert, was far too pretentious to make any for us.

Eric used his coffee-making skills to attract women. They loved it when he made it for them. The way they giggled when they saw the little milky heart on the cappuccinos he brewed was horrible—like five-year-olds who had just scored some helium balloons.

Eric had been with SHOW for four years and seemed somewhat tired of his job. He talked slowly, like a zombie, and it was hard to find joy in his eyes. The guy looked miserable; he reminded me of the flight attendant who had served me whiskey on the plane. Other people on the team wondered why he didn't quit if he was so depressed.

I knew that the coffee ritual gave him joy each morning, though. It put him at the center of attention and made him feel appreciated. We all told him that his brew was amazing and that he should quit to open a small café so he could chitchat with thirsty coffee lovers.

On this chilly October morning, Eric served my double espresso with a spoonful of warm skim milk on top. Gabe got a regular espresso without milk. Two girls I didn't know were served cappuccinos with hearts on top. As they walked away, I suspected they both had crushes on Eric. Eric himself was drinking a double. Sometimes he drank two in a row.

We took a seat by some windows in the café that faced the street and another office building. We could see straight through into offices opposite. There were piles of paper on the workers' desks and a small kitchen with a coffee machine. A red vending machine with a Coca-Cola sign stood in the corner. A bald guy in suit pants, a white shirt, and a black tie approached the machine and looked it up and down. He put his hand in his pocket and started to shake it around like something was itching him; then he pulled out some coins and counted them in his hand. Then, he threw his head backward like a barking dog. He left with quick steps and kicked the bin next to the door on his way out.

Everyone at our table laughed. Obviously, at that company they had to pay for their drinks. We were happy. We felt better and smarter than the bald guy across the street. He was probably miserable at work; maybe that's what made him bald, the stress of not having enough coins to get a Coke.

After we discussed how much we enjoyed our own excess of benefits and trash-talked random companies, a more important subject was raised: the upcoming Halloween weekend. With Friday being payday, there would be a lot of cash floating into the spending-spree account.

Eric told us with excitement that he was going to treat himself to a new Omega watch, but nobody really cared. At that moment, a guy came into the cafeteria. I'd seen him a few times around the office. He was short, about five foot six, and had curly brown hair that hung almost to his shoulders. His Levi's jeans were worn out and had some holes in them. I couldn't tell whether it was a fashion thing or he just lived a hard-knock life. His shoes were dirty, like he'd climbed up a muddy slope on his way home from the bar the night before. He looked tired, and I guessed he'd been in a long meeting since he had his laptop under his arm.

"Hey, Eric, can you make me an espresso? You're so good at it," he said in a mock-serious tone.

Eric snickered. "Sure, Alex. I'll make you a double—you need it. Guys, have you met Alex? He's a senior fox at this place." Eric went to the coffee machine.

Alex scanned us all from head to toe like they do at airport security before he introduced himself. Eric served Alex his espresso.

"What's this crap, Eric? Don't I get a heart on top like the girls?" Alex said with a slice of irony in his voice as he left.

"Not even a thank-you. What an asshole," Eric muttered as he came back to our table.

"Seems like a nice guy. Maybe he had a rough morning with meetings." For some reason, I jumped to Alex's defense.

"Meetings? Are you freakin' kidding me? He just came to work." Eric stared at me like I was moron.

Apparently Alex was a walking legend. He had played all the tricks in the book and constantly came up with new ones.

Each day he came to the office around ten or eleven in the morning, leaving his jacket on a floor below his own. He then came in with his laptop under his arm to create the illusion he'd been busy in meetings all morning—the trick I'd just fallen for.

Once he had told his manager that he is Jewish—which he's not—so he could get the day off on the next Jewish holiday. "God bless religion," he'd said with a smile.

He played his clients as well. He'd told an advertiser that he was an engineer and just answered yes to all their questions when they needed his advice about a technical implementation. When months later it turned out nothing worked, Alex said they must have done it wrong.

"The world is full of idiots," he'd said to his manager when asked why the client stopped spending money at SHOW.

According to Eric, Alex did these things because he loved to push the limits and win against the system. It gave him the satisfaction his work did not.

It was eleven o'clock, and we had to get back to our desks to do some work before lunch. On my way, I passed Alex sitting in a red beanbag with his computer on his knees. He had a bowl of potato chips next to him.

"Hey, you. Vic, right?" He looked up from his screen while chewing. "Let me show you something. You see these chips I have in this bowl here?"

I nodded politely, wondering what his point was. I noticed he was watching football on his screen.

"Well, you see, I've crushed them in pieces, so now I have at least twice as many." He waited with a sly smile for me to praise his brilliance.

"Wow, that's great, man. Enjoy," I answered and continued toward my desk.

9

Leakers get fired. These were the words in the subject line of an e-mail from our founder and CEO, Tim Nelson, on Friday morning. Some fools had been leaking client information to a random guy in a bar the night before. What they didn't realize was that he worked at the firm they were talking about. They were fired the next day.

When I had read the e-mail, I'd thought about how I supposedly worked with the brightest of my generation. Everyone had gone through multiple interviews and had degrees from top schools and a wealth of unusual life stories. Yet somehow idiots like the leakers passed the selection process and were told how special they were, that they were the one in ten thousand to get the gig. They were unique, yes. Uniquely stupid. Luckily it was Friday, payday—probably the last for the uniquely stupid—and Halloween.

That evening, I sat in a downtown movie theater, kicking off the Halloween weekend with the new James Bond movie. Suddenly someone from the front row in the movie theater hollered, "Fucking James Bond!" interrupting my thoughts about the e-mail and taking my mind back to the movie. Bond had just won $10 million in poker with a beautiful woman by his side, but everyone's eyes were now drawn from the screen to the bottom right row of seats.

It was Alex. He wore round sunglasses like John Lennon and sat there slurping a supersized soda while throwing popcorn into his mouth. I was sitting a couple of rows behind him with Hank and Daniel. We were all wearing tuxedos in honor of James Bond and Halloween. I saw Alex refill his supersized soda from a bottle of cognac, which could explain his outburst. We could hear him mumbling while he nourished himself with the drink and the movie continued.

Twenty minutes later, just after a sex scene, we heard a slow clap from the front row. "That's it. I am out!" Alex yelled, still clapping.

He tried to get up from the seat but fell back into it. During a second attempt, he put his hands on the armrests and lifted himself up, stumbled forward, and then lurched out the exit door. We noticed he'd matched his round sunglasses with gray boxer shorts, a white wifebeater, a black trench coat, and Nike sneakers. He looked like a psychopath and a molester all in one. God knows what he was trying to accomplish with that outfit or who he wanted to portray.

From the movie theater, we headed straight to a Halloween party in Mission Bay hosted by someone Daniel knew at SHOW. On the way, we bought a bottle of whiskey and a case of beer. Daniel also bought a bottle of red wine. He said it was good to have for the ladies, or in the worst case as backup fuel for himself if he ran dry.

At the party, we met catwomen, nurses, and Playboy Bunnies. Halloween was the one time of year women could dress as sluttily as they wanted and not only get away with it but get compliments for their wonderful costumes. For the guys, it was a chance to become Batman or Superman for a night.

The apartment was nice. It had a view of the bay and the stadium. It had an almost too clean design, with all-white decor. It felt like a hospital, like it had lost its soul. Fortunately, there were pumpkins lying around and black paper skulls hung on the walls and in the windows.

The smell of weed hovered around circles of people. There was a group constantly gathering around two guys. They seemed to be popular, but I didn't know why and didn't really care. I saw Hank standing in the kitchen making drinks. He kept spilling on the floor when he tried to pour, so I went over to stop him from wasting the whiskey.

A Playboy Bunny and a naughty nurse came over to us. They were disgustingly drunk and could barely stand in their high heels. Neither Hank nor I was interested in talking to them and told them we had to go. We wandered to the living room. There was still a gathering around the two guys, and Daniel was trying to cut in to get to them. After he'd talked to them, he came over and told us they were drug dealers. Then Daniel saw a Bunny and jogged after her, bottle of wine in hand.

Hank and I couldn't stand the shit-show party anymore and left for a club downtown, even though we weren't big fans of dancing. We drank and partied there for a few hours. When we walked out at around two o'clock in the morning, we saw Alex outside, still wearing his molester outfit. He was pacing back and forth and moving side to side like something bothered him.

"Hey, Alex, what's wrong?" I said.

"I really need to take a fucking leak right now! My bladder is killing me," he answered in a panic.

"Oh, well, just go behind a bush or a tree."

Apparently it was more urgent than finding a bush, which wasn't that easy in downtown San Francisco. He started a clumsy run toward the corner of the street, his steps wide and his arms held up halfway, like he was trying to balance on a tightrope. All of a sudden, he stopped. Then he turned around with his eyes wide open as if he'd seen a ghost. There was a big stain forming on his boxer shorts, beginning at his crotch and turning into a waterfall down his left leg.

"I couldn't hold it," he said without any embarrassment at all.

"No shit," Hank shouted and laughed.

"Leakers get fired!" I screamed.

As it turned out, leakers don't necessarily get fired. Not that night anyway.

10

Back at the office on Monday, I had lunch with Daniel and Hank. You could tell it had been an eventful Halloween weekend. The cafeteria was crowded with hungover, tired employees, all shambling around like the living dead and reflecting back on what had happened the previous nights.

Hank showed us photos he'd taken that weekend on his iPhone. He was extremely good at photography, and as with his coffee, obsessed with it. Many of the pictures he took were candid. Every now and then, someone would notice he was taking photos and start yelling and calling him a fucking creep. That was one of the reasons his images were so good. He captured the true reality of life. He hated taking shots that were staged or in any way planned. Once, a woman he'd taken a picture of while she made a ponytail in her hair had screamed she would call the police.

While scrolling through the pictures from the weekend, we saw a lot of Playboy Bunnies dancing, people drinking shots, and couples making out. There was also a picture of a smiling Alex standing on the street in his molester outfit with his legs wide open and a big stain on his boxer shorts. He'd said it was good that it happened because he was cold and the piss helped him feel warm for a while.

After going through all the Halloween photos, I began flipping through pictures of clothing on Hank's phone. I asked him why he had so many pictures of them. It turned out that he was a clothes dealer. He was as passionate about fashion as he was about coffee and photography. I remembered the two stunning designers who'd bought us whiskey and taken pictures of Hank at the bar our first night. I guess that explained it. A big chunk of Hank's paycheck each month was allocated to expensive clothing. Sometimes he spent it all and barely had cash to buy groceries, so it was lucky we got unlimited free food at work. To maintain his fashion addiction, he often resold the items after using them awhile. Daniel and I learned that there was a community of people buying and selling high-end fashion goods, trading them like stocks. Hank told us it was like a drug to him—even more so than smoking or drinking coffee.

Daniel was extremely interested in hearing about the clothes trade. He sat with his eyes and ears wide open, asking questions while I went to get us some dessert—blueberry cheesecake. Daniel had a nose for business and was always looking for new opportunities. To afford dating lots of women, driving monster Jeeps, and skydiving, he needed an extra income source. Currently, he was a domain shark, buying Internet domains at a low price and then selling them at a higher price. Usually he bought addresses with names similar to or the same as those of small businesses that didn't have websites. He then contacted the companies and said he could sell them their own domains.

"I've actually found a new area to trade in: camels," Daniel said with a grin when I got back with the cheesecake.

"Camels? You mean the animals?" I asked.

"Yep, the ones with humps on their backs," he answered proudly.

"You're such a hustler."

"I met a guy in a bar the other week who was doing it. I have to do some research, but it sounded good."

"Speaking of camels, how did it go with that tall girl at the party, Daniel?" Hank's mouth was full of cheesecake, and he had crumbs in his thick beard.

"Ah, quite good. But I made the mistake of offering her some weed," said Daniel as he turned his head to glance at a woman passing our table. "She couldn't really handle it and vomited off the balcony."

"That must be the one spewing in the picture I took." Hank laughed so hard the cheesecake crumbs flew all over the table.

"I bought it from the two dealers at the party, the ones that run their own little show, you know."

"What show? What do you mean?" I asked him.

The two dealers ran a personal enterprise within SHOW. They provided the entire company with drugs—you wanted it, they had it. They were both skinny and looked quite normal, nobody you would pay any special attention to on the street. They worked in sales, so they had the skills to sell their product. On the other hand, the demand was high, so they didn't really need to do much. It was like selling ice cream to kids on the beach on a hot summer day.

They were obviously smart guys and had figured out that they didn't need to do it all by themselves, since they could outsource and build a sales team that would do their shit for them. They now had a sales team of about five people who distributed their stuff around the office when they didn't do it themselves, like they did at the party. Different departments, different floors, different groups of people. And the two guys were just collecting the cash.

Every time I saw someone smoking weed or doing coke, I thought of John and got scared. I wanted to blame them for his death. Seeing them made me feel sick. I wondered what would happen if I punched them straight on their coke noses. I decided they weren't worth my attention.

We finished the blueberry cheesecake and went back to our desks.

11

I sat at my desk sending e-mails to clients, trying to schedule phone meetings with them so I could pitch new ad campaigns and get them to spend more money. Simultaneously, Hank and I watched funny cat videos.

Just as we were watching one of a dog chasing a cat in circles inside a bouncy house, I saw something, or rather someone, out of the corner of my eye. Everything stopped. I no longer cared that the stupid dog punctured the inflatable building with his sharp nails and got stuck inside while the cat escaped and left the dog to its fate. Hank was laughing like a circus clown, but I wasn't. I was too consumed by the moment to even tell him to shut up.

She strolled across the office floor like a magnificent lioness casually prowling through the savanna, knowing all the lions were drooling after her. What first caught my attention were her spectacularly long, sexy legs. Then I saw her dark eyes. They were like cups of hot chocolate I could drown in.

There was something—I had no clue what—but there was something hiding behind those eyes. I wished I could bottle the feeling and store it in a safe for eternity.

I hid behind my computer screen, staring at her, watching her move, watching her smile. Suddenly she turned toward me. I panicked and quickly dived behind my monitor so as not to come across as a sleazeball. Unfortunately, trying to get away with it made me look even more like a creep—a creep with no courage. She noticed me, and our eyes met for two seconds, maybe even three or four. It felt like forever. She gave me a troubled little smile, and her facial movement reminded me of a person at dinner with their in-laws eating a meat loaf that tastes like your grandpa's old socks. Still, you smile and swallow and say it was delicious, after which they serve you an extra portion.

When she left, I just sat there in silence, dazed. It was the first time since my ex-girlfriend had left me that I'd been so taken by a woman's presence. It bothered me. When Amanda had broken up with me, I'd decided not to fall for a woman that easily ever again. And it had worked. But now, with just one unpleasant smile, this woman had fucked up my mind and severely threatened my safety wall. That meant that she had the power to do more. I decided I would avoid her.

"Hey, you!" I said to Hank as I returned to my senses and awakened from the moment. "Stop watching those stupid fucking videos. Let's go for a coffee break."

"Yeah, sure. But this one is so good. Just watch it now before we go."

I leaned over and turned off his screen without saying a word. I think he got the memo.

12

As I walked to the office one December morning, the rain poured down as if the weather god were crying. Christmas was just around the corner, and it was the end of the sales quarter. People at the office were getting stressed about meeting their sales target but also excited for the upcoming holidays and the yearly SHOW Christmas party and gift. Everyone made guesses about what we would get. Rumors swirled: some thought it would be a smartphone, while others anticipated an Amazon gift card.

I'm usually not a big fan of Christmas. In fact, I hate it: the decorations, the stupid music, the presents. The expectations are always so high, and everything has to be perfect. My mother would always start getting stressed about four weeks before the holiday. She would run around like a lunatic to make sure everything was ready. Food and drinks had to be bought, the house cleaned, decorations prepared, and presents wrapped. If even one thing didn't turn out as planned, she went crazy. I never understood the point of it all. The duties took over the joy.

Usually, all the families in our neighborhood had big get-togethers at their houses or happily jumped in their cars and drove away to parties elsewhere. My childhood friend Chris had always gone with his family to visit relatives in Santa Barbara. I was jealous. I also wanted a big family gathering to go to, mainly to relieve stress and smooth things out. The more people around, the less anxiety. You could always escape and hang out with someone else.

I later learned that these outings were not as fantastic as I had thought they were as a child. Chris's dad, Patrick, was in the movie industry. He was an executive at a film studio in Culver City, Redlight Pictures, and worked a lot—and drank a lot. It wasn't uncommon on weekends to see him passed out on a chair by the swimming pool with a bottle of whiskey. We didn't really understand that it was bad; we thought he was just tired after work.

One Thursday, when Chris was sixteen, his father walked out. Chris, his younger sister, Nathalie, and their mother, Jane, were left alone. Nobody knew why his father left, and nobody asked. They just accepted it.

I couldn't really relate to it as a kid. My father had never lived with us. Growing up with only my mother and older sister was normal for me. When Chris's father left them, I told Chris he was lucky that he had at least gotten all those years with his dad. I thought this was extremely smart reasoning for being only a teenager at the time.

Our family in LA was small. There were only three of us—four during Christmas. Me; my mother, Wanda; my sister, Emma, who was five years older than me; and my father, Larry. We never went to any dinners and never had any at our house. This made me hate Christmas more and more each year. There was no fun in it for me, only pain.

"It's here!" I heard a girl yell from her desk like a crowing rooster.

I had just gotten to the office and was sitting at my computer typing in my password. I logged in, and the e-mail revealing the Christmas gift was at the top of my in-box. I looked across the office floor at the land of desks, observing the reactions of people when they opened it. Some were happily smiling and high-fiving. Others were swearing and saying it was the biggest scam of the year. I guessed it must have been the Amazon gift card. Well, not everyone is a fan of shopping—too bad for them. I opened the e-mail:

Subject: Your Christmas gift has arrived

Ho Ho Ho,

Merry Christmas, and thank you all for a great year. You can pick up your top-of-the-line phone tomorrow by the medical center.

Don't forget to call your loved ones and wish them merry Christmas!

Secret Santa

It was a phone, a brand-new one. For me to keep. I was amazed. At the same time, it bothered me that not all my colleagues were happy; on the contrary, they were angry. Disappointed. Furious. They walked around trash-talking the gift and spreading their dissatisfaction. They had gotten a phone last year and wanted a laptop this year.

It seemed like it was only the employees with seniority who complained, the ones who'd received SHOW Christmas gifts before. I felt sorry for them. I wondered what caused them to react so negatively. How could they be disappointed? Were they so spoiled and overtaken by greed that they needed more? They were getting a new phone, and meanwhile my friend back in LA working in a bank got only a box of chocolates to share with his coworkers.

I promised myself to never end up like them, not finding joy in anything. Poor bastards.

13

It was Friday, December 19, and time for SHOW's Christmas party, which everyone was excited about. This was the big chance to get drunk and go crazy all night long on the company dime while pretending the next day didn't exist.

When I got home from work around five o'clock, I dug around in my closet until I found what I was looking for: the black costume that would make it happen. I hadn't worn my tuxedo since Halloween, and now it was time to dust it off and let it turn me into James Bond with a license to drink.

I poured myself a whiskey and drank it in the shower. I pulled on black underwear, black socks, the black suit pants, a white shirt, and a black tie. I tied a pair of shiny black shoes, and it was time for the grand finale: the jacket. I looked at myself in the mirror and gave myself the classic eye-fuck, then finished off my whiskey, and left.

Outside on the street, I saw Bob in his checked flannel shirt and jeans mumbling and swearing about something as usual, holding a tool case in his right hand. The smell of smoke hit my nose like stinging hot sauce from a burned burrito. I saw smoke and its closest family member, fire.

The reason for Bob's swearing was now clear to me. Someone had lit a trash can on fire. Probably just some young kid having fun, maybe the future mayor of San Francisco. Who knew?

"Good evening, Bob!" I called out.

"Oh, hey, Victor. Do you see what these idiots did? Trash can is burning. People are so stupid these days!" Bob looked like he wanted to kill someone.

"Yeah, that's horrible, Bob. Fucking kids. Try pouring some whiskey on it." I grinned.

"That would be a waste of whiskey. I told the Chinese guy in the restaurant up the street to run and get some water."

"Good man, Bob, you're a good man. Enjoy the fire, and have a nice evening." I began walking toward Valencia to hail a cab. The guy from the restaurant came running past me with a bucket full of water. Bob followed after him to make sure the job was done properly and the fire put out.

After spending thirty-five minutes in a cab on traffic-jammed streets, I finally arrived at our regular bar, Rickhouse, to meet the guys. It was a typical bar for people from SHOW. A lot of us went there on weekends and after work.

The first thing that greeted me as I entered was the smell of liquor, perfume, and food. Lounge music played, and the laughter of excited people didn't really match the tunes. Everything was as usual.

A group of seven or eight women all dressed up and ready to party sat at a table right by the entrance. Their makeup was on, their hair had been through a couple hours of work, and their skirts were short. They sipped cocktails while laughing and glancing around to see if they would get any looks to boost their confidence for the night. Their phones were up, and the picture taking was intense. The competition for online attention had started—ready, set, and collect.

"Hey, Vic, over here!" I heard someone shouting from the bar. It was Daniel, sitting alone on a bar stool with a drink.

I glanced at the women as I passed them on my way across the room to him.

"Hey, man, what's up? Are you the first one here?" I asked, and then caught the bartender's eye and pointed at Daniel's glass to get the same liquid treatment.

"I sure am. Sitting here enjoying the whiskey."

We took a seat at a table by a window facing the street. The bar was starting to get crowded with more women ready to party and more men ready to take them on. A lot of familiar faces could be seen everywhere, mainly people from work. I saw Hank through the window, standing outside inhaling the very last of his cigarette before he came in. I waved him over. He noticed the same group of women as I had.

"Ah, come here, my bearded friend. How are you?" I gave him the whiskey I'd ordered for him.

"I'm great. Excited about tonight. It'll be a proper show," he said while scanning the bar.

"Yeah, I'll show the ladies who's the alpha male in here," Daniel said.

"Hank, have your camera ready. I'm sure there will be great pictures, as always," I said.

Twenty minutes later, Gabe rushed through the door. He looked mad. His glasses were wet, and he took them off and wiped them with a blue silk handkerchief. He was soaked, and his hair frizzed out into bush.

We waved him over to our corner, hoping he would see us, but the crowd blocked his view. He stood by the entrance for a while, searching the scene until finally we made eye contact.

"Hey, Gabe, how's the rain treating you?" Daniel asked with a grin when Gabe arrived at our table.

"I hate it. I'm all wet now, and my hair is a mess."

"Remove the tampon and cowboy the fuck up," Hank said. He spit some peanut shells into a glass.

After some drinks, Daniel ordered an Uber car to take us to the Christmas party. This year, the shindig was taking place in an almost-abandoned shopping mall on the corner of Fourth Street and Mission Street. Only the movie theater was open during the week, and SHOW had rented the entire building for the party.

The car stopped just outside the entrance. Each time the doors to the mall opened and someone walked in, the sound of music drifted out. We stepped out of the car and headed through the entrance. The main hall was enormous, and there were two bars on each side. A DJ stood on a podium, and there was an ocean of dancing people in an area in front of him that had been transformed into a dance floor.

People were riding up and down the escalators to all five floors. I could see waiters circulating with food trays on every level. Everything you needed was there, all served and prepared. The partygoers were acting like wild pirate kids in a candy store, plundering the food and drinks like there was no tomorrow. We went straight to the bar on the right side, ordered a round of drinks, and checked out the crowd.

Everyone was there, including Alex, the king himself. He was standing at the other side of the bar holding two drinks, one almost empty. I could tell he was already wasted, and he had a devious expression on his face. Shit was about to go down. He had a plan; God only knows what it was.

"Hey, Alex," I shouted when he came stumbling toward us.

"Hey, fuckers! What's up? Are you ready to get fucked up tonight? I sure am!"

He was wearing a black suit, black sunglasses, and a red tie to spice things up. His hair was neatly combed, and he looked like he had traveled back in time and just arrived from the sixties advertising world with a bottle of whiskey coursing through his veins. Hopefully he had located the toilets this time and would avoid a repeat of the Halloween incident.

"There they are, the little lords." Alex held his arms up toward two guys, trying to point them out with the drinks in his hands. "I just shopped a little from them. Special prices tonight."

He was pointing at the drug dealers, the two guys I had seen at the Halloween party. Both wore black tuxedos. They were shaking a lot of hands, exchanging a lot of hugs. Alex continued to ramble about everything, including girls, drugs, and his hangovers. I couldn't stand his bullshit any longer and went to the toilet to get some peace. I did that every now and then at parties when I felt suffocated. Sometimes at these kinds of events I'd just had enough—especially talking to random people I barely knew. They bored me most of the time. It was a pain and an effort to suffer through talking to them.

When I came back, Hank and Daniel were gone, and Gabe was still hanging out by Alex. I knew Gabe hated listening to Alex—couldn't stand it—but he was too kind to just leave. Instead, he stood there and watched the pile of shit coming out of Alex's mouth, nodding and smiling politely.

I saw a waiter with a tray of bacon and cheese sliders. I caught up to him and had retrieved three of the little burgers when I saw Eric. I walked over to him and a blond girl who was stuffing a slider into her mouth with both hands. She was pretty—probably his latest cappuccino catch, scored with the heart made of milk.

"Hey, Eric, no cappuccinos tonight?" I said.

"Hey, Vic, no. Tonight it's only gin and tonic—without the tonic." He laughed at his joke. "Have you met Jenny? She works in the finance department."

"Pleasure to meet you, Jenny from the finance department."

"I'm sure it is," she answered.

I left them and hurried back to Gabe to save him from Alex. Gabe was a good guy—too good sometimes—and didn't have balls when he needed them most. As Hank politely put it, he really did need to cowboy the fuck up sometimes.

"Alex, a woman is asking for you. Jenny from finance. Very pretty," I said. "You should go talk to her."

"Reeeally? Where's that beauty?" he slurred.

"She's standing with Eric, eating sliders." I pointed toward Eric.

"Eric? The cappuccino monster. Fuck that, I'm going over there." He gulped his second drink and pushed both glasses into Gabe's chest. Then he left, zigzagging through the crowd toward Eric and Jenny.

"Thanks, Vic. I was about to leave and head home," Gabe said.

"No worries. It'll be good fun when he gets to Eric and the blond. Let the cockfight begin."

Suddenly I felt a hand grab my ass. As I turned around, I saw a big beard. It was Hank, sipping his drink and holding his right hand on my ass.

"Can't find any girls that like you?" I said.

"Nope, no cunts, but I found some weed."

"Congrats. Now you should find someone else's ass to molest."

He laughed. "Maybe I will. I just saw Daniel chatting up a brown-haired chick at the bar on the second floor. He was even drinking a cocktail. What an idiot."

"It's an interesting word, cocktail. And cockpit, they both contain the word cock, as in penis. Isn't that fucked?" I asked Gabe and Hank.

"The world is full of cocks. Speaking of cocks, turn around and look who's on the dance floor with the brunette now," Hank said.

Gabe and I turned around and saw Daniel with a tall woman. When we had been roommates at Harvard, Daniel had always said his moves showed that he was the alpha male. I generally disagreed, although I rarely joined him at clubs to witness the action. To me, what he did didn't really seem like dancing at all. In fact, he reminded me of a poorly controlled marionette. As we watched Daniel trying to impress the ladies, Hank took pictures with his phone. Nicky came over to us, accompanied by a short brunette.

"Yo, Vic, what's up? Awesome party! Don't you love this?" she said. Her eyes were bloodshot. I'd seen her talking to the drug lords earlier in the evening.

Nicky was an intense person—a fully loaded battery pack, always talking and laughing. There was no stopping her. Instead, she calmed herself down with marijuana. She said it helped her come down to the same level as her surroundings, which was why she usually smoked a joint before her client meetings.

From time to time, she got so stoned that she didn't know what was going on. During one business trip to San Diego, Nicky had been smoking and drinking in her hotel room with two colleagues. They were all three on the sofa, and the other girl was sitting on the guy. The two of them were fucking, but Nicky didn't notice what was going on and kept on talking as usual. They told her the day after, but she didn't believe them. She'd told me the story several times and wanted me to agree that it would be too fucked up for them to have had sex next to her. She wanted someone to tell her that they were just joking. I didn't. Instead, I told her they probably liked the excitement of her being next to them and that she should ask if she could join next time—if she wasn't too stoned to notice, that is.

Nicky's dark-haired companion stared at me as I talked. She looked familiar, but I couldn't recall where or if I'd met her before. By that point I'd had a lot of drinks, and it was dark. When Nicky unexpectedly stopped speaking to chase after a guy who passed us, her friend took my hand and dragged me to the dance floor. I felt like a prisoner. The woman seemed to be determined to get what she wanted. I chugged the drink I had in my other hand and dropped the glass on the floor. It shattered into pieces.

The dance floor was crowded, with barely enough space to move. Hands were everywhere, and people constantly bumped into me. It was like a crowded cage of animals—all drunk, horny, and invincible. The music was so loud, it made the floor vibrate, the words disappear, and the heartbeats drastically speed up.

Out of nowhere, the brunette grabbed me by my shoulders, stood on her toes, and pulled herself up to lick me in the ear. Then she yelled that we should go home together. We left the party and took a cab to her place, which was just a mile away. She was wasted and so was I. It was not a love story, just a drunken story about desire and human needs, about sex.

We woke up together. It was warm. My mouth was dry, and my head pounded. The woman opened the window next to the bed, and the fresh air saved me from passing out. Everything in my head spun around like a carousel. I stared at the ceiling, hoping to find a point to focus my eyes on. There was a tiny, round black stain to the left of the lamp, and I stared at it to try to still the constant swirl in my brain. The girl asked if I was feeling okay, and if I wanted some water. I said I was fine, but I'd love some cold water. I watched her crawl out of bed and go to the kitchen.

While she was in the kitchen, I looked around the room. It was clean and tidy, with white walls and black curtains. Red roses stood in a blue vase in the window. Photographs of her and what I assumed to be her family hung in a circle pattern on the left wall, and in the middle of the circle was a photo of a man in his thirties.

The bed sheets smelled of laundry soap, and they felt fresh, almost like new. They seemed luxurious compared with my own, which I hadn't washed since I'd moved into my apartment in October.

She came back with the water, and I gulped it down. I could feel every ounce of it running through my chest, oiling up my inner system. We talked for a while, mainly her talking about how fun the night before had been and what an amazing company SHOW was, while I focused on the small mark in the ceiling and pretended I was feeling great.

To be polite and to act interested in what she was saying, I asked her how long she'd worked at SHOW.

"Eh, well, as long as you, since we started on the same day," she said.

Then it hit me. I knew why I recognized her. She was the one who had been sitting on my right during the welcome dinner, the rude blond who didn't want to talk to me: Chloe. She'd dyed her hair a dark-brown color.

To change the subject, I asked her about the photos on the wall. They were indeed of her family, but she didn't say anything about the man in the center. It seemed like she skipped him on purpose, trying to avoid mention of him. It was impossible, though. I was staring at the photo, so I asked her about it.

It was her ex-boyfriend, she claimed. She'd told him to leave three days earlier. They had been together for ten years. Now he was still calling her. Sending her flowers. Poor guy. She'd jumped into bed with me only three days after leaving him. Here I was, lying in bed with her, smelling the flowers he'd sent. If he only knew.

"If he only knew," she said with a sly smile.

"Yeah, I guess he wouldn't be so happy about this."

"Oh no, he would love this. He used to push me to it," she said happily, like it was obvious.

"Really? He liked you to fuck other guys?"

Apparently her ex-boyfriend urged her to cheat on him, encouraged her to have sex with others. Chloe told me he loved it; it was his weird fetish. It turned him on, knowing that someone else was in bed with her. He was also with others, sleeping around as much as he could, even though Chloe didn't like it. He claimed it was only fair. She didn't like him being with others, nor did she want to be with others herself. She did it only for him, to satisfy him and his desires. She was afraid to say no, afraid he would leave her. Her feelings all those years had been too strong to leave him, just as they were too strong to take the photograph down from the bedroom wall. Through it, she could still let him watch her having sex with others. She was doing it all only for him.

"Sounds a bit crazy." I was confused.

"Yeah, I guess. That's why I left him. Couldn't stand it any longer. When the affair with our parents took off, I'd had enough."

"Affair with your parents? Do they also cheat on each other?" I had a feeling I knew what her answer would be.

She turned away from me and pulled the white duvet over her body. I could see only her neck, where a five-pointed black star was tattooed. She was quiet for a while. I focused on the stain in the ceiling, waiting for her to answer.

"With each other," she whispered. "My father and his mother. They slept together. Several times."

"Sorry to hear that," I said.

"That's life. Do you have a girlfriend?"

"No, I wouldn't be here with you then."

"Why not?" she said. "Are you a saint or something? People cheat all the time."

"I don't."

"How do you know? Have you ever had a girlfriend?"

"Yeah, once. One day she just left." I was trying to figure out an escape plan. "Sorry, I have to go. I promised to help a friend with his car."

I looked at my watch. It was eight thirty on a Saturday morning. She didn't accuse me of lying.

I dressed, wished her merry Christmas, and left.

14

I was sitting at San Francisco International Airport drinking a latte and waiting for my flight to Los Angeles. It was early in the morning two days before Christmas Day, and I was on my way home to my mother. I watched the airplanes in the fog through the big panoramic windows.

I found airplanes insane—it was almost ludicrous that it was possible I could be thirty-five thousand feet up in the sky, sitting in a chair drinking coffee, reading a book, or watching a movie. The fact that it was all happening at the speed of about five hundred miles per hour made it amazing.

A silver American Airlines jet emerged from the thick mist and slowly rolled toward my gate. The staff on the ground, in their yellow jackets, were ready to welcome it. One of them directed the plane with his arms, finally making a stop sign by crossing both of his arms above his head. The aircraft stopped. The luggage and cargo staff advanced quickly with their trucks; the off-loading operation had started. The magic moment when the ground staff controls the big aircraft with their hands had come to an end.

Although I only had a one-hour flight ahead of me, I decided to stroll around in the terminal to stretch my legs before boarding. I saw a couple of familiar faces from the office around, but nobody I knew personally.

A woman with two carry-on bags hurtled toward me through the crowds in the terminal. When she got closer, I saw who it was—my always-stressed manager, Louise. I had never seen her walk. She always ran at the office, and now she was running at the airport. She zipped past me, calling out "Merry Christmas, Vic," and continued through the crowds. The departure screen indicated that the American Airlines silver bullet that would take me home to Los Angeles was ready for boarding, so I went back to the gate and boarded the plane.

My aisle seat was in row nine, very close to the front. It gave me a good view of the kitchen and the flight attendants. I always requested the aisle seat so I could stretch my legs out. Neither the flight attendants nor I appreciated it when they came through with the drink cart and ran over my feet.

Once in my seat, I noticed a flight attendant coming out of the cockpit. She was beautiful: tall with dark hair and brown eyes. She wore red nail polish and lipstick, all in sync with her red scarf. She had a smattering of freckles underneath her eyes, like a small army in a messy formation guarding her eyes.

The passengers boarding were in the way, disrupting my view of her as she stood in the front of the cabin welcoming them on board. I couldn't stop staring at her.

When the plane started to taxi from the gate, the safety demonstration began. Never in my life had I paid that much attention to this part of the flight, yet I couldn't recall a single word of it later. I was too consumed by her mesmerizing beauty.

Once the plane was airborne and had reached cruising altitude, the flight attendant directed the drink cart toward my legs. Row by row, she approached my seat. My heart began to pound when she reached row eight. I looked at her freckles as she served a bald man in the seat in front of me. I could see only the shiny top of his head. Once he got his coffee, she moved the cart one row down to mine.

"Good morning, sir. May I offer you some tea or coffee?" she asked.

"Coffee please, with milk." I didn't really want any since I had just had one before boarding, but I saw it as a chance to keep her standing by my seat a bit longer. "So, do you fly to Los Angeles often?"

"Every now and then. My boyfriend and I go there to surf." She gave me a big smile and handed me my coffee before she moved on.

Maybe she had a boyfriend, or maybe she had lied just to get rid of me. I could only hope her boyfriend had the same fetish as Chloe's.

15

I was standing outside the terminal at LAX waiting for my friend Chris to pick me up. The sun was shining on the chaos around the terminal; people were scrambling around with bags, and drivers fought for parking spaces. The leaves on the palm trees moved like the sails on the many boats in the San Francisco Bay Area. An airplane crew passed me by, the captain and copilot in front and the flight attendants behind them like a chain of baby ducks following their mother.

In the very back, I saw her: the woman who'd served me coffee on the flight. She yelled good-bye to her colleagues as they walked to the cab stand; then she ran toward a man with curly blond hair standing by a red Mustang. She jumped into his arms and kissed him passionately. Apparently she had not been lying about the boyfriend, though if the man with curly hair was her brother, I'd pass anyway.

Cab after cab approached me to ask if I needed a ride. I got sick of answering that I was waiting for somebody and started to ignore them, staring at the palm trees moving in the light breeze. I couldn't really blame them, though. Chris, who would pick me up, had asked me to wait by the taxi stand. He said it was a trick he does at LAX.

Finally an old silver Chrysler Sebring convertible stopped just in front of my feet. I was staring so intently at the palm trees, I didn't even notice at first.

"My man!" Chris hollered from the car. "The dreamer from the tech valley!"

His dark hair was a mess, and in his wrinkled Rolling Stones T-shirt and dark sunglasses, he looked like he was fresh out of bed—probably with a woman. He took a last, deep draw on his cigarette before throwing it on the ground and jumping out of the car. It was smoked almost to the filter. Chris made sure nothing went to waste. He took my brown weekend bag, threw it on the backseat, and jumped back into the car without opening the door. I followed his lead and climbed in and put my sunglasses on.

I told Chris that I was taking him for brunch at Rose Café in Venice. He turned out of the airport terminal and drove north on Lincoln Boulevard toward Venice Beach. He turned up the volume on the CD player, the sound so loud we couldn't talk, but we didn't want to. Instead, we enjoyed the moment of driving with the wind in our hair and the words of Freddie Mercury in our ears. Luckily the horrible LA traffic had let up for the moment, and we were actually moving instead of standing still and inhaling fumes in a traffic jam.

Chris constantly changed lanes so as not to break our flow. He didn't even check the rearview mirrors; he maneuvered based on pure instinct and insanity. We passed taxi after taxi, convertible after convertible, SUV after SUV.

After four or five Queen songs, it was time to turn left off Lincoln Boulevard and on to Rose Avenue, where we were stopped at a red light. A guy carrying a surfboard crossed the street in front of our car and turned and stared at us.

"What's wrong? Don't you like Queen?" Chris shouted.

"Turn down the volume so I don't have to listen to your shit music!" the guy yelled back before going into a 7-Eleven on the corner.

The light turned green, Chris stepped on the gas pedal, and we turned left and headed west toward Venice Beach and Rose Café. I could smell the ocean, feel the breeze on my skin. Seagulls flew above the car. We were close.

We parked our car with the valet and walked inside to wait for someone to seat us. The place was crowded and filled with hungry LA folks. Waitresses ran around holding plates filled with pancakes, omelets, and burgers and carrying trays with coffee and mimosas.

"Hi, honey, table for two? The wait time is around forty-five minutes," the waitress said.

"Really? Are you serious?" Chris asked.

"It's fine. We'll wait. Can you give my best to your manager? I work at SHOW, and you're one of our clients," I said politely with a smile.

"Oh, really? Actually I'll try to rearrange and give you guys a table right away. Come with me, please."

She led us to a table outside on the small patio. A canopy protected the guests from the sun, although some of it came through and created bright sun spots on the white tablecloths. I immediately ordered two mimosas, before she even gave us the menus. She said she'd come back soon to take our order.

Once the waitress was back, Chris ordered an omelet as well as pancakes, while I ordered huevos rancheros and French toast. We both ordered cappuccinos and orange juice to augment the mimosas the waitress brought when she took our food order.

It didn't take long for our food to be served. We'd barely managed to finish the mimosas. I couldn't wait to eat my eggs on a crispy tortilla with beans, guacamole, and chili salsa. I loved my huevos rancheros at Rose Café, and every time I came home to LA it was the first thing I ate. Chris dug aggressively into the pancakes like it was the first, or last, thing he'd ever eaten.

"You like the pancakes?" I asked.

"Mhmm, amazing," he answered with his mouth full.

We ate and talked about old times. Memories from the times when everything seemed so easy and we had no real responsibilities, problems, or worries. We both laughed with our mouths full of pancake while remembering the time we, together with John, stole apples from my neighbor Mr. Gibbons. We'd been caught as we were filling up a plastic bag with the shiny red fruit from the tree in front of his house.

We talked about the times when we stood at Venice Beach Boardwalk, and Chris played the guitar while John sang lyrics I had written, and I collected cash in a hat from people passing by. Girls with sparkling eyes flocked around us. The boardwalk bar owners used to ask Chris to come play at their bars. I acted as the agent and arranged the gigs and handled the payment. We were a band with one guitarist, one singer, and one writer and manager.

When Chris's father, Patrick, left his family, Chris became even more dedicated and determined to succeed with his dream, which his father didn't support. Patrick had told Chris he should get a business degree and a proper job, like the one he had. Patrick had seen too many broken dreams in Hollywood throughout his career. These days, Chris had a real band called Stay Classy. They had gigs every now and then at different bars and clubs in LA, but they hadn't made it to the big leagues. Not yet.

Chris asked me how I was doing in San Francisco. I told him about my new life, how amazing it was to be a part of SHOW and the rapidly booming tech industry. I told him that it was the future and that I couldn't be in a better place.

He said that maybe he should reconsider and study business like I had, make money, and be safe. I told him he should follow his dreams and not what other people do.

"Let's not be like our dads, making a corporate career our goal and then fucking it up and finding ourselves alone," I said.

Chris asked what I did at the office when I wasn't eating the food, bowling, or drinking coffee. My answer was brief: nothing special or complicated. I sold ads to clients, the ads he saw when he browsed the Internet.

"Do you have time to write anything?" Chris said, his fork in midair.

"Nah, I haven't written anything since I left Boston."

"Shame. Write me some lyrics, man."

"I'll try."

Chris's mouth was full, and he nodded and gave me the thumbs-up with his left hand. "How about the ladies?" Chris said once he'd swallowed.

"They're okay."

"I hope you're not still thinking of Amanda."

"No, no. I actually saw a really nice girl at the office the other day. She was awesome." I smiled.

"Yeah, nice, man. What's her name?" Chris looked interested.

"I don't know. I didn't talk to her. But I really want to. She had something special." I took a sip of my coffee.

Chris laid down his fork. "Then do it, man. You have nothing to lose."

I shrugged. "I guess, except being rejected and having to see her around."

"Possible, but what if you don't get rejected? That's more interesting."

"You're right," I said, folding up my napkin. "I'll ask her out when I get the chance."

I asked the waitress for the check, paid it, and left her a good tip.

We left Venice and drove to the cemetery where John was buried. The three of us had been best friends growing up. After high school, John had moved to Connecticut to study finance at Yale, I'd moved to Boston to study business at Harvard, and Chris had stayed in LA to pursue his music dreams.

John had been offered a job as an investment banker on Wall Street a year before his graduation. The pay was good, and Wall Street was trendy. It was the dream of many finance students to work there. John found no reason to decline the offer. The Wall Street bank locked him in for the job at an early stage, and the risk of saying no was too big to take. Even though Wall Street wasn't his dream, getting the job calmed him; it was the easy way out.

But once there, he'd felt like a commodity, like a machine in a moneymaking factory. When we talked on the phone, he'd joke around that he had to hang up and get his shovel and go back to the money mine to start digging.

I had asked John why he didn't quit if he hated it. He'd said the risk was too big, and he didn't dare to. Without the job, he wouldn't be able to maintain the same comfortable lifestyle, with its fancy dinners and nice apartment in Manhattan with a view of Wall Street. He was so locked into the money digging that he had lost track of reality and couldn't quite figure out what was real and what was fictional gold dust. Wall Street was just numbers changing place.

Both Chris and I knew John wasn't satisfied. He'd told us as much when we'd visited him just after Christmas the previous year. But we hadn't realized how bad it was. He seemed happy, looked good, and had just had a first date with some girl from work. We knew he did coke every now and then with his Wall Street buddies to handle the pressure and the long working hours.

One Saturday morning, John had been found dead in his apartment by his housekeeper. He'd died alone in his living room with a view of the place that had ruined him. He had OD'd on cocaine and was gone forever.

John couldn't find any happiness in what he did. Two weeks before his death, his girlfriend had left him because he never had time to be with her, and when he did, he was usually on coke.

Chris and I both felt low after the visit to the cemetery, and we didn't talk in the car. Chris put on a Beatles CD and drove me straight home to my mother's. He left me on the curb with my bag, saying he was in a rush for band practice. He told me to wish my mom merry Christmas from him.

I stood on the street in front of my house for a little while, wallowing in the childhood memories of playing on the lawn, the smell of roses in the garden, and the sound of our doorbell ringing for a long time when John and Chris pressed the button together.

I looked over and saw our next-door neighbor, Pat Gibbons. His wrinkles were obvious, and he moved more slowly than usual. His right arm shook when he pulled the mail from the mailbox. He flipped through it and threw half of it into the trash can standing on the driveway. I noticed that his left arm also shook slightly.

As he turned around to go back to his house, he glanced up from the letters in his hand and noticed me. I said hi and asked how he was doing, but he didn't answer. He hadn't been a fan of me or my friends when we'd played around in the neighborhood. Maybe because we sometimes stole apples from his tree, which was now gone, or maybe just because he hated kids. I watched as he shuffled back up the driveway to his house and felt sorry for him. He was all alone.

My mother opened the door and yelled for me to come in. I paused to watch Mr. Gibbons close his door, then took my bag from the sidewalk and strode up to the house and into my mother's arms. She hugged me and kissed me. She asked how my flight was, how the food was, if I was tired, if I'd forgotten anything, if I was hungry or thirsty, if I'd brought everything, if I'd met any nice people, and if I wanted to go to the bathroom. She was a very concerned and loving mother. It was both wonderful and annoying as hell.

"Sit down. I've made meat loaf," she said.

"I just had brunch with Chris, Mom. He says hi by the way."

"You should eat anyway. They probably didn't give you enough to eat at the restaurant, and it's lunchtime." She guided me toward the table.

I sat down at the table in the kitchen, and she served me a plate of meat loaf with gravy—my favorite.

"Aren't you gonna have some?" I asked.

"No, no, I ate an hour ago. You go ahead and eat now. It's delicious." She sat down across from me with a cup of black coffee and poured two teaspoons of sugar into it.

We talked about the trip: everything had gone fine, and there were no delays despite the fact that it had been extremely foggy in San Francisco before my departure.

"Did you visit John?" she asked.

"Mhmm. We went straight after brunch." I poured more gravy on the meat loaf. "How have you been?"

"I'm okay. A bit lonely." Her voice was low. "And I don't see your sister much, unfortunately. She works lot. She also has a new boyfriend. Again."

"Well, that's expected. Have you met him?"

"No, I barely see her. All I know is that he's not from the industry."

Emma, my older sister, was working in the film industry as an assistant to a studio exec at Paramount Pictures. She'd always dreamed of becoming an actress. She ran around to different castings every week in the chase for her future Oscar nomination, but her dream was slowly breaking apart into small pieces, like an apple crumble pie, week by week, audition by audition.

Emma was just one of thousands in LA with broken acting dreams. The difference in her favor was that she could go back to her family home and cry. Those that came from far away didn't have that luxury and had to find comfort sleeping in a car or under a bridge. Emma's acting ambitions caused turbulence for all of us, but mainly for her and my mother, who had to take care of her and comfort her when she didn't get the parts she wanted. Sometimes she even threatened to kill herself due to the misery she suffered.

After eating, I told my mother I was tired and would rest for a while. She was headed to the supermarket to buy the last groceries for Christmas.

I picked up my bag and climbed up the stairs to my old room. I stood in the doorway and took in the sight. The window blinds were half down, and the sun shone into the room, creating a sharp shadow line on the light-blue walls. A poster of Wayne Gretzky in the LA Kings hung above the bed. On the other side of the room, my tennis racket leaned against the small wooden desk. The desk was empty except for a pen and a notebook.

Just above the desk there was a photo collage with pictures of me, Chris, and John. Some were of us at the Venice Beach Boardwalk; others were of us playing video games or splashing around in the swimming pool in Chris's yard. Chris and John had made it for me when I turned ten. It had been hanging in the very same spot since that day, beaming out memories for over a decade. It felt like time stood still in this room; everything was just as I'd left it when I went to Harvard.

I put my bag by the desk and lay down on the bed. The bed linens smelled of lavender laundry soap, the same soap my mother had used for as long as I could remember.

While lying in the bed, I looked at the photo collage and smiled, but a moment later my happiness turned into anger. I was angry at what had happened to John and that we could never update the collage with new photographs, angry that the Wall Street fucks recruited him and lured him into their devil's nest.

I took the stereo remote from the nightstand and turned on my old silver Sony stereo. I pressed the "CD" button, and John Lennon started to sing to the room. I closed my eyes and slowly drifted away to Lennon's words.

"Relax, Mom, who cares?" I heard my sister Emma yelling downstairs.

It was not my favorite voice to wake up to, but I was used to it. There had been years of screaming and arguing about bullshit throughout my childhood. Emma must have come home while I was sleeping, and my mother was apparently back from the supermarket as well. I assumed that my sister was complaining about something related to the food, which would have provoked my mother to fight back, saying something along the lines of it needing to be this way and that traditions were made to be kept.

John Lennon's voice was gone. All the CD tracks had been played. I must have slept for an hour and a half or so. Walking downstairs to say hi to my shouting sister, I felt like I'd traveled back in time and was ten again.

As I suspected, my mom and sister were standing in the kitchen arguing about food, in this case a potato salad. I said hi, we hugged, and I told them both to calm the fuck down and stop arguing. Emma called me a little shit and said that I should mind my own business and stop lecturing them. I told her to stop being a diva and tell me who her new boyfriend was instead.

"He's in real estate, West Hollywood. He drives a Porsche and has a hot tub in his house," she said proudly.

"Wow, that's great. What a prince. You should marry him tomorrow."

"Fuck you. You're so bitter." She stormed out of the kitchen.

"So, is Dad coming over for Christmas this year?" I asked my mother.

"He claims that he will, but you never know," she said.

My father lived in New York City, and although he was still married to my mother, they had never lived in the same city or even the same state. Most years during my childhood, he'd come and visit us in LA at Christmas. Sometimes we flew to New York to visit him instead.

Until he'd retired a few years before, he had worked as an art director. The job consumed so much of his time and attention that he hadn't gotten married until the age of fifty, and even then he had never lived with his wife or kids because of his career and life in New York.

Each summer break from school, I was sent to New York to spend a couple of weeks with him. The heat was horrible compared with LA. It was humid, and there was no ocean breeze. The air stood still between the skyscrapers. I could barely stand it and prayed for rain every day.

When I was a kid, my friends all thought my parents were divorced since I lived with only my mother. When I told them my parents were still married, they all asked what I meant and how that was possible. I just told them it was fucked up, and there was nothing I could do about it.

I heard a car honking outside on the street. It was Chris in his convertible.

"I'm going out for dinner and drinks with the guys from high school," I said to my mother as I put my shoes on.

"Don't stay out too long, and don't drink more than two drinks. And don't forget to eat before you drink. Don't forget it's Christmas Eve tomorrow."

"Yeah, yeah, don't worry so much. Relax. It's not like the president is visiting."

"Take a banana with you so you can eat in the car." She came running with a banana.

"No, thanks, I'm good. I'm going to dinner."

She forced the fruit on me, and I took it on my way out the door. I walked over to Chris's car, jumped in, and asked if he wanted a banana. He stuck it in the glove compartment and started to drive toward the restaurant in Santa Monica where we would have dinner before going to a club in Hollywood.

16

The next morning, I again woke up to the sound of my sister yelling. It was Christmas Eve day, and I could only imagine the stress being felt downstairs in the kitchen. I'd come home from the club around three o'clock in the morning after a quick visit to In-N-Out Burger for a couple of cheeseburgers. The cheeseburgers did me good. I had no hangover at all and felt fresh. I showered, dressed, and went downstairs to see what all the fuss was about.

Emma was crying, and my mother was comforting her. I asked what had happened, and Mom said that Emma's boyfriend was supposed to visit today, but he'd broken up with her over the phone this morning.

My wish for a peaceful holiday did not seem likely to come true this year either.

"Vic, your father called earlier this morning. He's arriving at LAX at four twenty-five on United, terminal seven. Can you pick him up, please?" My mother gave Emma a new tissue.

"Sure," I said.

* * *

At four o'clock, I took my mother's white Tesla and headed to the airport to pick up my father. I crossed Olympic Boulevard and drove on to the Santa Monica Freeway before hitting the 405 South, where I got stuck in traffic. I was already annoyed that I had to drive to the airport, annoyed at Christmas, and annoyed at meeting my father. I turned on the radio and calmed down.

All the radio channels were flooded with shitty commercials about Christmas and consumption: buy this, best value, gift of the year. I switched the station and managed to hear some music between the ads; as soon as one started, I changed stations.

I was a bit nervous about meeting my father. I felt like I had a big hard stone in my stomach, and there didn't seem to be much chance of it disappearing. The same feeling struck me every time I saw him, probably because throughout my life I'd seen him only once or twice per year. Each time it felt like we had to get to know each other as if it were the first time all over again—a bit like a first date. It usually took two or three days of spending time together before I relaxed and felt comfortable with the fact that it actually was my father I was talking to. Then once that feeling came, he left, and months would pass before I saw him again.

I arrived at LAX about thirty-five minutes past four and pulled over at terminal seven, where loads of people were coming out and being greeted by those waiting for them. As I watched the automatic glass doors of the terminal building open and close, the stone in my stomach changed in density with the movement of the doors.

After waiting for ten minutes, the doors slid open and my dad came out. The stone in my stomach exploded, easing my anxiety a bit. He looked a lot older than he had when I'd seen him a year earlier. The sun reflected off his gold watch. He dragged a black suitcase on wheels with his left hand and carried a plastic bag in his right. As usual, he wore khaki pants with a white shirt tucked into them.

He stopped outside the doors for a moment and then headed toward me once he spotted me. I stepped out of the car, hugged him, and asked how the flight was before I opened the trunk to put his suitcase in.

"It was okay—not as okay as before. They make you pay for drinks these days."

"Mm, yes, it's tough to run an airline nowadays."

"Well, they still keep the airfares high. They just wanna make more money. Greedy management."

We jumped into the car, and I started to drive out of the terminal toward the 405. I told my dad about Emma's boyfriend, saying that he was supposed to have come over today but they'd broken up.

"You know her," I said, "constantly having new boyfriends. She should take a break and be single."

"Agreed. The most important thing is to be able to date yourself, then you can date others. At the end of the day, you can only trust yourself." He put on his sunglasses.

I drove way above the speed limit, nearly eighty miles per hour, wanting to get back home as soon as possible and take the burden of being alone with my dad off my shoulders. Forty-five minutes in a car was a long time for a first meeting after so many months, especially without my mother there to break the ice.

My father and I pretended everything was normal, as if I'd just picked him up after a short business trip, as if we lived together as a family, as if we had ever lived together as a family.

We arrived back at the house at around five thirty, and I parked the car in the driveway. My father went inside while I took his bag out of the trunk and locked the car. On the front stoop, I took a deep breath. "Merry fucking Christmas, Vic," I said to myself, then opened the door and entered the yearly holiday show.

17

Roast turkey, ham, goose, mashed potatoes, and gravy. It was time for Christmas dinner, and everything was on the table as it should be according to my mother's tradition. She dashed in with the roasted root vegetables and put them on the table, at the same time shouting at my sister to keep an eye on the pumpkin pie in the oven.

My mother's grandfather was of Polish ancestry. During World War I, he served in the US army. She always followed her grandfather's traditions, which is why she also served a stuffed carp and herring in cream sauce on the Christmas table. Her grandfather had also passed on the tradition of leaving an empty plate on the table for unexpected guests that might be wandering around alone on the streets. I always hoped that someone would show up outside our house and join us to release the tension of the forced family dinner. It never happened.

At eight sharp my mother said it was time to eat. We sat down at the well-laden table, wished each other a merry Christmas, and put our forks into the cold cuts. It was important to eat in the correct order, and my mother managed the process like an assembly line in a factory.

"I'm so proud of Vic getting that job at SHOW." My mom put herring on her plate. "Larry, you know it's almost impossible to get a job there. They only hire the smartest students."

My father didn't seem to be listening; he was occupied with some herring.

"Vic, tell your father the percentage of applicants they hire. I've forgotten," she said.

"They only hire point one percent of the people that apply," I said.

"Yes, that was it. Only point one percent. I'm so proud."

I knew that even though my father had been an art director at an advertising firm, he wasn't a fan of global multibillion dollar companies. He always said that it was different: he was an artist. Creating something beautiful demanded hard work, talent, and creativity.

"Of the ones that apply," my father said. "How many apply?"

"I don't know, thousands," I said.

"So, what exactly do you do?"

"Sell ads. I call clients in my portfolio and pitch advertising campaigns. Sometimes we meet in person."

"Do you have a girlfriend?"

"No." I thought of the girl I'd seen at the office just before the Christmas party.

"Why? You should get one. It's important, so you don't end up alone." He took a sip of his wine. "The older you get, the harder it will be. You need to think of the future and a family, not just play around at work."

"It's not like he can just get some random girl," Emma said.

"I'm just saying so you don't end up like me, old and alone," he said.

"Mmm, the herring is so good. It's fresh. More wine anyone?" my mother asked.

My father was turning eighty next year. His life and career in New York City had postponed his family plans and made him a father late in life. My mother met him in New York during a business dinner with her father, who ran a shipping company in Long Beach harbor. My grandfather's company was a client of the advertising agency my father worked at. The plan had been that he would move to LA, but it never happened.

When we were done eating, I took out the trash, and on my way back in I saw Mr. Gibbons sitting in his kitchen window, facing the street, alone. I asked my mother to put some ham, goose, and mashed potatoes with gravy in a box for him. I'd go and give it to Mr. Gibbons and maybe talk with him for a couple of minutes. In a second box, I put some stuffed carp and herring. Then, I wrapped a piece of pumpkin pie in a napkin and put it all in a white plastic bag.

My mom said it was noble of me and hugged me. She was a woman who loved to help others and never thought about herself. She'd lived her entire life through others' happiness and success.

The door was old, and the white paint had started to fade, leaving empty black spots, reminding me of a cow. I pressed the metallic button to the left of the door and heard the bell inside the house. Nothing. After a minute or so, I pushed it again, and once more I heard the ringing. I knew Mr. Gibbons was in there since I'd just seen him ten minutes before.

Finally I heard noises coming from inside, and the sound of boots against a wooden floor became louder and louder. Then the lock clicked and the door opened. Mr. Gibbons stood on the other side of the doorsill.

His thin gray hair was well combed, he was clean-shaven, and his thick, gray eyebrows were furrowed above his confused eyes. His blue shirt had stains on it, just beneath the collar. I could smell liquor; he reeked of whiskey but didn't seem too drunk. He stood straight without swaying.

"Hi, Mr. Gibbons. I just came by to wish you a merry Christmas. I brought some food that my mother cooked. It's delicious. Are you hungry?"

He stared at me, then reached out his shaking hand and took the bag of food. "Thank you. Come on in," he said.

The furniture inside was old; you could tell that an old man lived there. The place was neat and clean, not like the bachelor pad of a young college grad. We went through the hallway into the kitchen. A half-empty bottle of whiskey stood on the table by the window. There was one empty glass next to the bottle.

"Are you old enough to drink? I recall you as a young boy." He looked at the bottle.

"I am," I said.

He opened the glass cabinet and reached for another whiskey glass. His hand shook, and he flipped the glass on the floor. It smashed into small pieces.

"Fucking shit," he said.

I saw a broom in the corner next to the fridge and moved to sweep up the glass. He thanked me, reached for a new glass, took a seat by the table, and started to pour whiskey into it, spilling a bit on the table. He then filled up his own glass.

"Cheers!" he said.

As I drank, I noticed that he spilled a bit on his shirt each time he moved the glass to his mouth. His shaking hand did not make life easier.

We talked for a while. He told me his son had moved to China to pursue a career years before. He had never come back and still worked as a manager at some company there. Didn't have a wife or any kids, just worked all the time. Married to his job. Didn't even have time to come to LA and visit.

Mr. Gibbons himself had worked at the US Post Office; he had been an area manager for many years. Striving for advancement, he'd worked long hours and finally gotten promoted to city manager. Two years later, his wife had left him, saying that he only cared about the post office, that his job was more important to him than she was. The years he'd spent chasing promotions had slowly broken their relationship. He didn't realize it until it was too late. One day he'd come home from work, late as usual, and she was gone. Just like that. He heard from someone that she had moved to Palm Springs and found a new man there.

"Never marry your job, kid. It won't last forever." He finished his drink.

I emptied my glass, wished him a merry Christmas, and went back home.

Two days later, I said good-bye to my family and flew back to San Francisco and SHOW. Christmas was over for this year, and it was time to once again sell ads, drink, and party.

PART 2

1

"That's it, I'm out!" Alex shouted loudly and got up from his office chair. "Hurry up, guys, the wine bottles are limited. I hate it when they run out."

"Yeah, yeah, take it easy, you dolt. Go ahead and grab us a table," Daniel whispered. He had a client on the phone.

Alex called him a fucking amateur and then headed toward the cafeteria where the wine was waiting. It was Friday afternoon and, same as every week, the FridayShow was about to begin. This Friday was special, though: it was New Year's Eve.

Alex was a man of many talents, but responsible drinking was definitely not one of them. He drank a lot and often, and once he started, there was no holding him back. At every FridayShow, he grabbed two bottles of red wine for himself. Then he sat and drank them both in one go, without standing up. By the end, he would begin to sway a bit in his chair.

Today's FridayShow was no different. When we walked into the cafeteria, he was sitting with two bottles of red wine and waiting for us at a table. Daniel grabbed two bottles of Bud Light; he knew Alex would not let us in on his wine.

"So, you guys know where they serve the best wings in town?" Alex asked.

"Hmm, Kezar Pub," Daniel said.

"Fuck no, amateur!" Alex chugged his wine.

"Okay, so what's your place?" Daniel said.

"Dirty Habit. Next to Powell Street. The best!" Alex said.

He claimed to be a wings expert, like he was the only guy in the state of California who really knew wings.

"Let's try it someday," I said.

Hank came to our table with a bottle of sparkling wine and some plastic glasses and sat down. He opened the wine and poured everyone a glass. "They've just filled up all the fridges with sparkling."

"Where's Gabe?" I asked.

"He went home to his chick. They're hosting some fucking romantic couples' dinner," Hank said.

"What an idiot. Fucking pussy." Alex reached toward the bottle of sparkling.

"Fuck no, you mooch." Hank grabbed the bottle before Alex reached it. "Go get a new one."

Alex put both of his hands on the table and pushed himself up from the chair before he stumbled away into the crowd to find some sparkling.

"That guy, he can be such a cunt sometimes," Hank said.

"While he's gone—dinner and drinks at my place at eight?" Daniel said.

"Sounds good," I said.

"Perfect, and then the party," Hank said.

A friend of Daniel's roommate, Jules, had invited us to a New Year's Eve party he was hosting at a new club downtown. Jules worked in a cocktail bar in the marina and was well connected with party people. He often brought girls back home for drinks when his shift was over. Daniel found that very convenient and said it was better than pizza delivery.

Nicky passed our table with a bottle of sparkling and sat down once she saw us. "Hey guys, happy New Year's!"

"Hey, what's up, Nicky?" I asked.

"I was just heading over to the girls over there." She pointed at a table a few rows behind us. I turned around. Two girls were waving to Nicky. I felt a stone form in my stomach: one of the girls was Chloe and the other was the tall beauty I had seen at the office before Christmas.

"Oh, so what are you guys doing tonight?" Hank said.

"We're going to dinner at Maggie's place and then to a house party in Sausalito. You guys should join!" Nicky said.

"Sounds fun, but we have plans for dinner and a club opening," I said.

"Hey, how's it going with that sparkling, Nicky?" Chloe and the beauty appeared beside our table. Chloe introduced herself to Daniel and Hank and then turned to me. "We've already met, at the Christmas party right?"

"Yeah, we did."

"I'm Maggie," the tall beauty said.

"Maggie joined SHOW and my team just before Christmas but missed the party," Nicky said.

"Yeah, I had to fly back home to my parents in New York for my dad's birthday," Maggie said.

"Girls, let's go. I wanna have a glass now." Chloe pivoted to walk back to their table.

"Have fun tonight, guys," Nicky said and left with Maggie.

I hadn't known that Nicky and Chloe knew Maggie. I wondered if Maggie knew I had slept with Chloe after the Christmas party. I wondered if that fucked up my chances of getting a date with Maggie.

* * *

We left the office before Alex came back, planning to meet up again at Daniel's place in the Castro for dinner. I arrived there at eight o'clock, and Hank arrived a half hour later. We'd meet Jules at the club later.

Daniel had made a three-course dinner for us, including lobster, steak, and chocolate mousse. We drank Bollinger champagne with the lobster and Chivas whiskey with the rest. Around eleven, Daniel ordered an Uber car and we headed to the club.

I pulled my phone out from the inside pocket of my black blazer and saw that I had four new text messages. My mother, Chris, and Gabe all wished me a happy New Year. There was also a message from Alex saying that the party he was at was shit and he wondered where we were. I wrote him back that we were going to a club on Ellis Street. He wrote that he'd be there in thirty minutes.

We arrived outside the club and were greeted by a drunk Jules as soon as we stepped out of the car. We walked in with him via the VIP entrance. I told him a guy named Alex would show up any second and that they should let him in. Jules told the bouncer to write it down and let Alex in when he arrived.

Inside, Daniel and Jules immediately started chasing girls, while Hank and I went to the bar to order whiskey sours. I wondered if it was stupid of me to decline Nicky's invitation to join the girls at the party in Sausalito. It would have been my chance to talk to Maggie. If I'd only known that Chloe and Maggie were friends, I never would have slept with Chloe.

"Heey guuuys, what's up?" I heard Alex calling behind me.

He had managed to get in despite being stoned and drunk as fuck. Hank said he had to go and take a leak. I knew he was lying.

Alex ordered a round of rum and Cokes and launched into an anecdote about how he once bought cocaine from a prostitute in Las Vegas. In the middle of his story, I heard a countdown from the speakers. There were ten seconds till midnight, and there I stood, listening to an alcoholic talking about hookers and cocaine.

"Well, cheers, you bore!" Alex screeched as the countdown reached zero.

"Happy New Year!" I said along with the entire club.

"Alex, Alex! The cab is here! C'mon!" Daniel shouted while holding a cab on the street in front of the nightclub.

It was two thirty in the morning, and people were everywhere in the street: drunk girls in high heels were running around like deer on ice, and drunk guys were chasing them like starving hyenas. I sat in the cab with the door open while Daniel yelled at Alex to get in. I hadn't seen Hank since he left to take a leak when Alex arrived.

"Hi, I'm Alex," I heard a woman's voice say from outside the cab. Suddenly she jumped in to the cab and sat next to me in the backseat.

"Well, okay. Please, help yourself then," said Daniel with confusion. Then he shrugged his shoulders and jumped into the cab.

Instead of our friend Alex, we ended up driving to Daniel's apartment with an unknown woman whose name was also Alex. She was attractive, tall with dark-brown hair and a nice figure.

The cabdriver pulled over outside Daniel's apartment, which was just next to a gay strip club. "That's twenty-five bucks, guys," he said with a smile.

"Here's thirty. Keep the change." I gave him the cash and opened the door.

"Thanks, man, enjoy your night. Sharing is caring." He laughed an evil laugh and gave a dirty old man's leer. He could have played Shrek.

Daniel opened the door to the building, and he, the mystery Alex, and I walked up two flights of stairs to his apartment. He had trouble putting the keys into the lock and fumbled with them for a while before he managed to open the door. On our way to the living room, we passed Jules's bedroom and saw that he was already sleeping.

The three of us took a seat on the white couch standing by the wall in the living room. The windows were open, and there was a cool breeze from outside. We were all too tired to move from the couch and close them.

Daniel was cold and wrapped himself in a red blanket lying by the couch. Being a real proper gentleman, he didn't offer the blanket to the unknown Alex, who sat in her dress, freezing.

My phone rang, and I took it out of my blazer and saw it was our Alex. I walked to the kitchen to talk to him. He wanted to know where the fuck we were and said that he'd bought some cocaine. I told him we hadn't been able to find him and that we'd see him on Monday at work. *Fucking cokehead,* I thought to myself.

I opened the fridge. Inside there was a shelf filled with Bud Light, a bottle of sparkling water, two cans of Coke, a Snickers bar, and a pack of hot dogs. I took the Snickers bar and went back to the living room. Daniel was wrapped in the blanket and passed out snoring on the couch. Our new friend Alex was gone.

Out of the blue, I heard moaning from Jules's bedroom. Apparently he was not sleeping anymore. I opened the door slowly and peeked in. Our new friend Alex was on top of Jules, taking a ride. Jules saw me peeking in and smiled. He looked like a kid on Christmas Day. He was very grateful for our mistake and made us pancakes for brunch the next day. Still smiling.

2

At the end of January, Daniel and I were sent on a business trip to LA to meet with one of the biggest clients in our portfolio, Redlight Pictures, a film studio in Culver City. We were supposed to present them with a brilliant advertising strategy—which we should have been developing during the last week—wine and dine them, make them buy in, and then fly back the next day. On Monday, the night before the trip, we sat in Daniel's apartment preparing the presentation when Jules came back from work with four girls. Our work night turned into drinking games with the girls. As the games moved on and we got drunker, Jules disappeared with one of the girls into his bedroom.

Kimberly, a tall blond with a tattoo of some Asian signs on her left wrist, sat next to me on the living room couch drinking Jameson.

"This tastes like shit," she said.

"Nobody is forcing you to drink."

"I was a marketing intern at a fashion company once. The founder, Ben, always drank Jameson. His fucking wife hated it." Kimberly poured herself some more. "She went to my mom's yoga classes in Sausalito and gossiped about him."

"You have any blow?" Kimberly's drunk friend yelled from the kitchen.

"No, we don't have any fucking blow. Do we look like coke-heads?" I shouted back.

"Chill. Don't be rude," Kimberly said. After a minute of silence she said, "Lucky for you, you turn me on, so I won't waste this fine glass of whiskey by throwing it in your face."

She then chugged her glass, leaned over, and kissed me. A minute later we left and took a cab back to her place in Noe Valley, had sex, and fell asleep.

The alarm on my phone rang at five thirty in the morning, and we both woke up. I started to get dressed.

"Are you fucking kidding me, five thirty?" Kimberly yawned.

"Have a flight to catch," I said while I put my T-shirt on.

"Sure."

"It's true. Client meeting in LA."

"Ah, of course, you work at SHOW. Forgot. I actually know a girl who works there. We're in the same yoga class. Maggie. You know her?"

"Nope. We're a big firm. I have to run. Sweet dreams."

Fuck. I had slept with another one of Maggie's friends without being aware of it.

I could only hope that Kimberly was not a gossip girl and that they weren't close friends.

I left Kimberly's apartment and took a cab back to mine. I had the cab wait while I ran up, packed my bag, grabbed my laptop, and ran back down.

Our flight was scheduled to depart from San Francisco at seven thirty, and by seven o'clock, I was waiting for Daniel at the gate, drinking a double espresso and observing the planes.

"Hey, Vic!" I heard someone holler.

As I turned around, I spilled some coffee on my white T-shirt. Nicky was standing behind me.

"Hey, Nicky, what's up? Are you going to LA too?"

"Yeah, we're flying down for a client meeting with Louis Vuitton. You know my colleagues, right?" She smiled.

Two other women were behind Nicky, and my heart stopped for a moment. One was Chloe—and the other was Maggie. I couldn't help staring at her once again, like a creep.

"Hi, yeah, we met once," I said.

"Hi, Vic, what's up?" Maggie said.

It was an awkward moment: I didn't know what to say; I was too awed by her. My brain stopped functioning. She had done it again, violated the wall that was supposed to keep me safe from women coming too close. I still had no clue how she did it.

I told them that I had to go and find Daniel and escaped into the bathroom to call him. He didn't answer the first two times I called, but on my third try he finally picked up the phone.

"Where are you? We're supposed to board soon," I said.

"Heeey, maan. Chill chill chill, no stress," he said.

"I'll see you on board," I said.

"Yeeep, I just have to finish this baby." He hung up.

As I walked back to the gate from the bathroom, I heard our names being called out through the speakers in the terminal. When I reached the gate, I realized that everyone had already boarded, so I did as well, hoping that Daniel would make it.

Just as I buckled up in my aisle seat, I saw him coming in through the airplane door, smiling at the flight attendant. He took the seat next to me and buckled up. We had a one-hour flight to prepare our presentation for the client.

* * *

We landed in Los Angeles at eight forty-five and took a cab straight to Culver City for our meeting with the film studio. We were still working on the presentation in the car on the drive, making up numbers that would sound good—numbers that we couldn't really explain or fully prove, but they were so good nobody would say no to them. Because we worked at SHOW, we knew the client wouldn't question them either. We were confident our fairy tale would work. It was an easy sell. We had observed our managers making up numbers for their bosses every day. The higher-ups were so overwhelmed with data that nobody ever questioned it. We figured we could do the same thing.

The cab stopped outside the studio entrance, and Daniel paid with his corporate card while I got out. The sun was shining, and the air was much warmer than in San Francisco. I was a bit worried about our meeting, but Daniel seemed to be relaxed and to not give a shit about it. "This is how you do it," he said. "Everyone is doing it. Just make things up; it's fairy dust."

We pushed through the glass doors into a room with marble floors and a giant mahogany desk. A receptionist in a blue suit sat behind the desk. Big movie posters in gold frames hung on the wall behind him.

"Welcome to Redlight Pictures. How may I help you gentlemen?" he asked.

"We're from SHOW, here to meet Angela Schwartz at ten fifteen," I said.

"Wonderful. Please register your name on the screen over here." He showed us a touch screen.

We entered our details, and a small machine standing next to the touch screen printed us personal visitor tags. The receptionist took them and put each one into a small plastic cover attached to a lanyard.

"Please wear these when you are in the building and return them to me when you leave. Please go to the fifth floor. They will meet you there. Have a nice day." He smiled.

At the elevators, I pressed the button with an arrow pointing up. It illuminated, and the doors opened just seconds afterward. Inside, I pressed number five on the keypad.

"I'm high," Daniel said.

"What?" I said.

The elevator stopped, and the doors opened. A woman in her thirties wearing a dark-blue dress and high heels stood just in front of us. She had red hair, green eyes, and freckles on her cheeks.

"Hi, and welcome. Angela," she said, putting out her hand.

"Hi. Victor." I shook her hand while looking into her narrow green eyes.

"Daniel." Daniel shook her hand.

"Pleasure. Let's go. The others are waiting in the room."

She led us into a conference room next to the elevators. There was a long wooden table surrounded by black leather chairs and a very large TV screen hanging on the back wall. Five middle-aged men waited for us. Around the table were water bottles, each with one tiny glass next to it. The huge windows on the right side of the door had a view of a garden and the hangar-like buildings on the premises. It was cold inside; the air-conditioning was really making an effort.

Daniel and I walked around the table and introduced ourselves before we took a seat at the end of the table, our backs facing the TV. Angela took a seat at the other end by the door. I poured us some water while Daniel told them that the flight was relaxing and we had enjoyed coffee on board while reading the newspaper.

It was now the two of us in T-shirts, a coffee stain on mine, in a room with six Hollywood execs. I was getting increasingly nervous and glanced at Daniel. He was leaning back in his chair, drinking water before the show began.

"So, Vic and Daniel are here to present an online marketing strategy on how we can market our movies premiering this Easter. We're listening," Angela said.

"We sure are. Let's start," Daniel said and fired off the presentation.

Ten minutes or so into it, the door opened and a man in a suit came in. He seemed familiar. He immediately took a seat by the door next to Angela. I looked more closely at him, and after a couple of seconds it struck me. It was Chris's dad. The asshole who'd left them when Chris was sixteen. I hadn't seen him since then, and I barely recognized him. He was skinny and pale. His eyes were dark, and he was almost bald. Our eyes met, and he quickly turned his attention to the papers on the table. I knew he recognized me. After two minutes or so, he left the room.

Five minutes later, we finished the presentation. They loved it, saying that they would commit to our proposed advertising budget of $400,000. Now we just had to take them to the promised dinner and drinks later that day so they wouldn't change their minds.

On the way out of their office, I called Chris and told him I was in LA for the day and suggested we should meet for lunch.

I took a cab from the meeting to the In-N-Out Burger on Sunset Boulevard in Hollywood, where I waited for Chris. I watched him arrive a couple of minutes later and park next to a police car. The two officers were sitting at the table next to me eating burgers and drinking shakes. Just as Chris entered, the officers got a 211 call on their radios, and they grabbed their shakes and rushed out. They were gone in less than a minute. Reading a lot of Michael Connelly's crimes novels had taught me that 211 was the code for robbery.

I told Chris to hold the table while I ordered burgers, fries, and milkshakes—chocolate for Chris, vanilla for me. Some things never change.

"The client meeting I just had, it was at Redlight Pictures," I said.

"Okay," Chris said and took some fries.

"Yeah, I was sitting in the meeting when your dad came in."

Chris took a bite of his burger and chewed slowly. Then he picked up his milkshake and drank.

"He didn't look good," I said. "More like he was sick. I thought that maybe you should call him and meet up. See if everything is okay."

Chris abruptly stopped drinking the milkshake and put it down on the table. His expression became concerned. "I don't know. He should call if something's wrong. We'll see. Anyway, thanks for telling me."

I told him not to act based on pride; it didn't matter who called first. After lunch, we hugged good-bye, and I took a cab to my mother's for a quick visit before I had to go back to the W Hotel in Hollywood, where Daniel and I were staying and would host the dinner for our clients.

Daniel and I met outside the restaurant at eight o'clock that night. A hostess in a black dress seated us around an oak table, and we waited for the studio people to join us. There were four solid silver candleholders in the middle of the table. I could barely see Daniel sitting on the other side. I asked the hostess to remove the candleholders since they were in the way, and she took them away one by one, grabbing each of them with two hands and walking over to a table nearby to put them down. Her nails were painted dark red, and she had a scar on her ring finger that was as long as the finger itself. On both hands she was slightly red and bruised around her wrists, which she tried to hide with a couple of gold bracelets on one wrist and a silver watch on the other.

She disappeared and came back five minutes later with the studio people, who must have been waiting by the entrance to the restaurant. Only three out of the six people we'd met with earlier in the day showed up for the dinner: two older men in their fifties wearing suits and Angela.

One of the men was bald, and I suspected the other one wore a toupee because his hairline now seemed lower than it had during the meeting. I didn't recall their names and hoped that Daniel would greet them by name. Then I remembered he'd been high during the meeting and probably didn't remember either.

Angela took a seat in the chair on my left and the two suits took a seat on either side of Daniel. We ordered a round of drinks. The men both ordered gin and tonics. Angela ordered a whiskey on the rocks, as did Daniel and I.

"Wow, Angie, whiskey on the rocks, eh? Can you handle it?" the bald one said.

The one with a toupee laughed. "Yeah, will you be able to find your way home later?"

"Yeah, you should stick to wine and water: the soft stuff, just like at the office," the bald one said.

"Andrew, watch out so the bubbles in your tonic don't hurt your tummy." She didn't seem too bothered by their bullshit and toasted with her glass of whiskey before taking a big sip and saying to the man with the toupee, "Oh, Ray, do you have a new haircut? You look different—good different."

The waiter brought our appetizers and two bottles of red wine, and around forty-five minutes later, the main courses arrived with another two bottles of red wine. We were all getting a bit drunk, especially the two suits, Andrew and Ray. They had been sipping gin and tonics between the wine.

I finally couldn't stand their drunk-talk anymore and needed a break. I excused myself and went to the bathroom. I went into a stall and sat on the toilet to relax. I checked my phone and saw a message from Nicky: she was at a client dinner in Santa Monica with Maggie and Chloe. She was high, and the dinner sucked. She asked if we wanted to meet up and party afterward.

I didn't answer. I didn't dare meet Maggie at the same time as Chloe, and I still wondered if Nicky and Maggie knew that I had slept with Chloe. Instead, I texted Chris and asked if he had called his dad. I waited ten minutes or so, but he didn't answer, so I went back to the table.

"Hey, junior, what took you so long? Can't you handle your whiskey or what?" Ray said.

"I thought I would give you guys the chance to rest," I said and sat down.

Angela leaned over to me and whispered in my ear that they were both fucking pigs and belonged in a zoo. I whispered back that I didn't think anyone would pay to see them; they'd be better off in a cave with Neanderthals. She laughed and finished her wine.

The waiter came in with desserts and cognac, and the dinner finally came to a close. When we were done, Daniel asked the waiter for the bill and paid with the corporate card. The bill came to $1,168, which Andrew saw. He patted Daniel on the back and said that their commitment to our budget proposal should cover that.

"So, Angie, want a ride home?" Andrew said.

"No, thanks, I'm good," Angela said.

"I have a new beauty, silver Mercedes-AMG," he said.

"But you drive it like a woman," Ray said.

"At least I know how to drive a woman. Angie, this is your chance," Andrew said.

"No, I don't care about cars. I'll get a cab."

The hostess in the black dress came and asked if we enjoyed the dinner. I said everything was great and thanked her. Andrew asked her if she was single and if she wanted to take a ride in a new Mercedes. She answered that she had a boyfriend, and Andrew said she should dump him and come along with him—he might have a role for her in an upcoming movie. The hostess said she wasn't an actress and wished us a good evening.

"Well, boohoo. So, you guys wanna go to a strip joint?" Andrew said. "Angela can take a cab home, and we can take my ride."

"Thanks, but we're good. Early flight tomorrow morning," I said.

He called us all boring fucks, chugged his cognac, said goodbye and left. Ray thanked us for dinner and left with him.

"Fucking finally!" Angela was drunk and spoke without restraint. "I hate dinners with that dirty pig, Andrew. Cheating on his wife and hitting on me every chance he gets. Reminds me of my father."

She put her hand on my thigh. "Let's go to a club and dance. It'll be fun. Some of my friends are out."

"Yes, sounds awesome!" Daniel answered instantly.

As we left the restaurant, we passed the hostess with the bruises on her wrists. I told her she should leave her boyfriend and nodded at her wrists. She nodded and said she knew she should. Then she gave me a polite smile.

We took a cab to a club on Sunset Boulevard where Angela knew the bouncer. We skipped the line, and a drunk guy called us fags. Daniel gave him the biggest smile he could.

We walked across the dance floor and up some stairs to a table where Angela's friends sat. The table had vodka bottles all over it. Angela introduced us to her friends and said that we worked at SHOW and we'd just had a client dinner with the dirty pigs from her office. Her friends laughed, but it was clear they felt sorry for her; it was caring laughter.

One girl said one of their friends worked at Louis Vuitton and was also out at a client dinner with people from SHOW; they might drop by. Great.

We had some drinks, and when the DJ played Jay Z's "Empire State of Mind" one of Angela's friends climbed up to dance on the table. A bunch of guys at the table next to ours started cheering and taking pictures with their phones.

Angela asked me if I wanted to go out for a smoke, and I followed her through the crowd to an outdoor bar and smoking area. I ordered two whiskey sours while she lit a cigarette. Although I still didn't know Maggie and hadn't spoken more than a word to her at the airport, I felt like I was cheating on her. I found myself surprisingly attracted to Angela—even though she smoked, which I personally didn't like—but something deep inside me was drawn to it. It created a mysterious sex appeal that became visible in the smoke around her.

I handed her the drink and she took a sip.

"What's wrong?" Angela asked me after she took a drag of her cigarette.

"Nothing."

"Come on, tell me."

"Tell you? What do you mean?" I said.

"Why you're so distant. Why don't you relax?"

"I don't know what you're talking about."

"Oh, come on. Cut the bullshit and tell me why you're afraid," she said.

"Takes some time before I trust people."

"People? You mean women?"

"Tell me why you didn't become a psychologist instead."

She laughed, took a deep drag of her cigarette, and then took a sip of her drink. "That was my father's job. So who left you?"

"This girl Amanda. We dated at Harvard. She left me on our one-year anniversary. I don't know why."

"She wasn't in love. That's life."

I said we should go inside again, and she kissed me on the cheek, then turned around and went in with her drink. I stood and watched her walk while I finished mine.

On my way back to the group, I bumped into Nicky on the dance floor. She was moving like a maniac and was higher than ever. I couldn't handle her right now, and I wasn't in the mood to dance, so I kept walking toward the table before I realized that Chloe and Maggie were probably also in the club.

As I approached, I saw them squeezed onto the couch by the table, drinks in hand. Maggie sat next to a guy in a red shirt who was flirting with her. She was laughing, and he kept touching her shoulders over and over. Every time he opened his big fucking mouth he leaned closer to her.

I couldn't stand it, but I didn't know what to do. Chloe was staring at me, and I turned around and started watching the dance floor. I saw Daniel dancing with Angela. She must have run into him after smoking on the patio. They were dancing pornily with each other. Suddenly she looked up and our eyes met. She gave me a flirty smile.

I left the club and walked back to my hotel, drunk and miserable and lost in thought: *No control. Total lack of power and rationality. The feeling, the unstoppable feeling that's impossible to fully tame, like a wild animal. You think you're in control, but deep down it's still a wild emotion that fucks you inside and out. It makes you lose your mind; it changes you as a human on this earth—a big nasty mindfuck.*

That's what it is. Some people refer to it as love. Love is painful. Love is loaded; it's a drug. We get loaded on the drug for free the first time, and it comes with your biggest hangover: a deep, black hole filled with emotion that you have to climb out of before you proceed to the second time to get even more loaded.

For some, the first time is also the last. No hangover; no deep, black holes; no mindfuck. Instead, it's a long joyful trip that might last forever. But it doesn't come without risk.

I lay down on the hotel bed and instantly passed out.

3

"Good job in LA, guys! I heard they committed to spend what you told them. Well done!" My manager, Louise, congratulated Daniel and me at lunchtime the next day when we got back to the office from the airport.

"Thanks. It was a fun trip. Good meeting," Daniel answered.

"Will definitely help hit the sales target," Louise said and ran away.

We left our bags and laptops by our desks and went for lunch with Gabe and Hank. The cafeteria was filled with black balloons, black cupcakes, and waiters walking around wearing black suits and pouring champagne. The balloons had the number ninety-three printed on them and so did the cupcakes.

It was the first Wednesday in February, and last year's earnings report for SHOW had been released earlier the same morning. The revenue result was $93 billion. SHOW had never made that much money in one year. We broke our record almost every year, and we were worth the celebrations and the cupcakes.

We sat down by a corner table with a view of the bay. A jazz band played in the other corner of the restaurant, and I saw Alex run after a waiter, grabbing two glasses of champagne from the tray and drinking one of them immediately and then exchanging it for a new one. He turned around, saw me eyeing him, and laughed.

He started to talk to the waiter, and then they both headed toward our table. Alex told us to grab some glasses from the tray and joined us.

"Aren't you eating? The lobster burger was great," I said.

"Nah, I'm only drinking today. We made ninety-three fucking billion last year. Everyone should just drink and chill. It's good for the fellowship and solidarity," Alex said.

"I've never agreed with you more," Hank said.

"Fucking Ryan! Look at him, the animal. He's a total predator." Alex pointed at a tall guy sauntering around the cafeteria with a glass of juice in his hand.

"I've seen the guy around the office a couple of times. Why's he a predator?" Daniel asked.

Alex told us that Ryan was constantly chasing women, like a hunter. According to Alex, Ryan was a sex addict and never gave up. He flirted with almost every girl at SHOW, and there was no "Off" button; he was unstoppable. If a woman denied him at first, he just got more motivated to get her into bed. He strolled around in circles on different floors in the office, hunting for potential targets to chat up. Instead of minding his sales targets, he spent half his days creating algorithms and action plans for each and every woman he talked to or planned to talk to. SHOW had taught him to be data driven and measure everything, and he really did measure everything.

"Are you drunk? What the fuck are you talking about?" Hank asked.

"Drunk?" Alex said. "I can do more than three glasses before I get drunk."

Alex told us that Ryan kept a record of every encounter he had with a woman and noted down how they responded to his questions. He collected data to learn what worked and didn't work. Everything came into play: environment, time of day, weather, his clothes, her clothes, her hair, what he said, what he did not say.

Everything. He then used all that information to optimize his flirting techniques for the best possible result. Every woman had her own file, in which he recorded the data. It helped him with his next attempt if he didn't succeed on the first one.

"It sounds fucking crazy, and it is," said Alex. "But it works. I've seen his files and data sheets. The algorithms even calculate a percentage chance of how likely it is that Ryan will get a date, get a kiss, or get laid."

"Fuck me, that's crazy," Hank said with salad in his mouth.

"And creepy," I said.

"Interesting, ambitious, and innovative. You have to give him that," Daniel said.

Maggie. I couldn't stop myself from wondering if he had a file on Maggie. I started to imagine that he had been dating her or at least had tried to. I wondered if he had kissed her, or worse, slept with her. Although I thought it was sick, I couldn't help but be somewhat jealous of his data collecting skills. I knew that knowledge was power, and information gives you an extra ace in the game.

Ryan had been working at SHOW for over three years, and data collection was priority number one at SHOW. It was ingrained in the employees. Everything was measured, both internally and externally. We were drilled to measure, calculating, crunching, and presenting numbers, figures, zeros, and ones. The data was the gold of the twenty-first century. Data mining had become akin to gold mining for our generation. We were the new "forty-niners," like the gold miners that had come rushing to San Francisco and California in 1849 to search for gold, mining incessantly for hopes of reaching the eureka moment. The difference was that we used computers and the Internet instead of shovels and gold pans.

SHOW measured the office's overall performance and compared it to the food they served to the employees in the office restaurants on a given day and then optimized the menu for maximum profit. The health center at the office compared your blood type to your performance, making it possible for SHOW to determine which blood types perform best at certain tasks and in particular roles—everything to improve the overall performance. Every detail mattered, and SHOW was extraordinary at making sure everything was taken into account.

As Alex talked, I watched Ryan approach a woman from behind. He slowly sidled toward her, carrying his glass and maintaining perfect posture. He leaned over her left shoulder, and I saw his lips move as he said something to her. She turned around with a confused expression on her face, gave him a condescending look, and said something before she strode away.

He'd been turned down, yet he didn't seem to care. He took out his phone and swiped his fingers across the screen. I could only assume that he was entering data in his file on that girl, taking a note on his action and her reaction to plan his next move.

4

On Tuesday morning the next week, I woke up with a headache and a dry mouth. I opened my eyes and stretched for my watch, which lay on the nightstand. I couldn't reach it. I had to turn over and roll closer. Once I managed to slowly lift the watch, I had to close my right eye and stare at it before I could focus and see that it was already eight thirty.

I walked out to my kitchen, opened the fridge, and looked for water. I couldn't find anything to drink in my fridge, so I turned on the tap and waited for a minute or so before I put my finger under it. It was cold, not ice cold but cold enough to drink. With a shaking hand, I rinsed a dirty whiskey glass and then filled it to overflowing. I immediately put it to my lips and drank and then drank two more glasses. I took two aspirins and then decided I didn't give a shit today and wouldn't go to work.

I went back to my bedroom, crawled into my bed, pulled the covers over myself, and slowly fell asleep to the sound of the veins pumping in my head.

I woke up sometime after lunch, around two o'clock, still feeling entirely trashed. I checked my phone and saw that I had a couple of missed calls and messages. Two calls from my manager, one from Daniel, two from Gabe, and one from Chris. Both Chris and Louise had asked me to call them back. I sent an e-mail to Louise telling her I was sick at home and would probably not be in the next day either. This hangover felt like it would last awhile.

I searched for pizza delivery on SHOW's website on my phone, and an ad for Domino's Pizza came up. I hit the "Call" button, turned the speaker on, and put the phone next to my pillow. I listened to the rain smash against my window while waiting for it to ring. Once it started to ring, I counted the rings until a guy named Jamie answered on the fourth one and asked how he could help me.

I told him he could help me by getting a pepperoni pizza to my apartment as fast as he could—I hadn't eaten all day and was starving. Then I added that I would pay in cash and tip the delivery hero generously if he came quickly. Jamie asked if I wanted a drink, and I said no and then quickly changed my mind and said I wanted a large Coke. When Jamie told me it would take about twenty-five minutes for delivery, I told him my dead grandmother would be faster than that. Then I reminded him that I tipped well and hung up the phone. I closed my eyes and fell asleep.

The knocking on my door woke me up. I didn't know whether I was dreaming or not; I never had unexpected visitors, and I was not in my full senses. I heard a thin voice yelling "Pizza delivery!" outside my door and remembered that I'd ordered food. I crawled out of bed and stumbled over to the door to open it. A short, blond teenage boy stood outside wearing a blue Domino's uniform. He was soaking wet. He gave me my pepperoni pizza and Coke and told me I owed him $15.99. I asked him if he had been standing outside my door for long, and he said that he had been knocking for at least five minutes or so. I took the pizza box and put it on the bed and then rummaged in my nightstand for cash. I found a twenty and a ten and gave it all to him.

"Keep the change," I said, "and don't share it with your manager."

I went back to my bed and opened the box. Steam smelling of pepperoni and cheese hit my nose. It was still warm, but not hot. I opened the Coke bottle and listened to the little bubbles fizzing inside of it. After a minute or so the fizzing began to subside, and after two more minutes it was almost gone. I took a big sip.

I put the bottle back on the nightstand and took a bite of the pizza. I ate one slice, and then I closed the box, put it on the floor next to my bed, and fell asleep again.

The next morning, I didn't go to work even though I felt fine. I decided it was a good day to be off, and I was sick of ads and numbers. Nobody was going to die if I didn't show up—I wasn't a heart surgeon.

I crawled out of bed, put on a pair of jeans, a black T-shirt, and dark-blue sneakers. I grabbed my wallet, phone, and sunglasses, and stepped out of my apartment.

My stomach aggressively demanded food by sucking out all my energy, leaving only a vacuum inside me. I stepped out of the building, and the first thing I saw was Bob standing on the stairs with a jar of paint and a brush. He was dirty, with green paint on his gray shirt and blue jeans. He even had paint on his face and in his hair.

"Morning, Vic. Beautiful day today, isn't it? Watch out for the paint," he said.

"Hey, Bob. Yeah, it's nice."

I was too tired to ask what he was painting and didn't care enough to look around to see for myself, so I just walked down the stairs and onto the street and kept going.

A little café called Magnolia was just five minutes from my apartment on foot and was one of my favorite spots for breakfast. Because I ate my meals at the SHOW restaurant, I rarely had food at my apartment. I didn't even know how much a gallon of milk cost, nor did I know the cost of a loaf of bread or a block of cheese in the local grocery stores; I never visited them. SHOW had extracted me from reality, but who the fuck wants to live in reality?

On weekends, Magnolia was always crowded with young professionals eating their hangover brunch and discussing all the fucked up things that had happened the night before. So many SHOW employees lived in the neighborhood that the SHOW drug lords often showed up there on Saturdays, allowing their customers to get cocaine with their eggs Benedict. Luckily, at ten thirty on a Thursday the place was almost empty.

I ordered a ham and cheese omelet, orange juice, and a cappuccino and took a seat at a corner table overlooking the street. I had never called Chris back, though I should have. I struggled to take my phone out of my jeans pocket while sitting on the chair. The waitress came with my drinks. I took a sip of the cappuccino, then of the juice, then of the cappuccino again. I pressed Chris's name on my phone screen, put the phone to my ear, and waited for him to pick up. I counted the rings as I always did. There were six before I hung up.

The waitress came by and said that they were out of ham. "That's a shame because I really wanted the ham," I complained. "I guess I'll make do with the cheese only. I'll probably survive without the ham."

I made light of it and said I was fine, but I was still annoyed. I took a sip of the cappuccino to calm down and tried to forget that I wouldn't get any ham in my omelet that day.

5

The next day, I was back at work and was in a meeting that was about a previous meeting, which we had had to discuss another meeting that we'd had in response to a meeting someone had had with someone else. Almost everyone in the room was sitting with their laptops open browsing the Internet, reopening the same websites over and over again to see if anything new had happened during the twenty seconds since they'd last checked.

My phone vibrated in my pocket. I slowly took it out and held it under the table to see what was on the screen. It was a text message from Chris. I opened it: *I called my dad. He has cancer. /C*

I wrote him back and said I was sorry to hear that and that he could call me whenever he wanted. He answered that he didn't want to talk about it now and that he'd call me when he was ready.

The meeting ended, and I went back to my desk without a clue as to what it had been about.

6

It was a Saturday morning in mid-March, and I was on a bench in Golden Gate Park absorbing the sun and people watching. I'd always found it relaxing to observe life and movement around me. Sometimes I even wrote about what I'd seen.

Cigarette fumes slowly floated in front of my eyes, the sunlight breaking the smoke into parts like a magical laser. It was a beautiful sight—smelly, but beautiful. The water in the lake was shining, like a mirror reflecting the image of the world: a world dominated by white ducks and swans, fighting over the territory. Just like humans, the birds marked off their land. We are all the same, all equally primitive.

A woman sat next to me on the bench watching the ducks and their war with the swans. Her nail polish was as red as blood, and her hair was as dark as the bottom of the lake. Her eyes were covered by opaque sunglasses. Her hand, with its red fingernails, slowly moved toward her lips so she could enjoy her cigarette, drag by drag. The smoke floated straight into my face, but I didn't mind. I enjoyed watching her in action.

To my left, I heard a constantly nagging voice. It was a woman in her thirties whining over the phone that her boyfriend had left her. Obviously it was not meant to be. And if it were, he would come back sooner or later.

The birds flew around like maniacs, chasing each other in circles and crapping all over the park. I saw a homeless man passed out on the grass about fifteen feet from me. He didn't notice when a bird took a shit on his face. Again, the birds marked their territory and attacked invaders in their park. Poor drunk, at least he was passed out.

The smoking woman and I gazed at each other. We connected; we agreed—we didn't say a word, but we agreed. She took out another cigarette without asking me if I wanted one. On top of that, she blew smoke at me, but I still liked her.

A really old couple passed by. I could see their wrinkled faces from a distance. The man was wearing a nice blazer, a proper one. It looked like he'd had some great times in it; it was an experienced jacket with stories of life. A lot of women must have fallen for him in that proper blazer back in the day. His old lady was probably one of them. She was wearing a black hat and that kind of dress only very old women wear, the kind of dress you can sometimes find in vintage stores around Haight-Ashbury if you're really lucky.

We were becoming a crowd. At first it had just been the cigarette woman and me. Then the whining woman had arrived. Later, there was the drunk man, and finally the proper blazer man with one of his success stories walking by his side.

The sun continued to cut through the cigarette smoke and shine on us. The woman's red nails were still as appealing as before, and I was thinking of ripping her sunglasses off to see what she looked like behind them.

That would be rude, but fuck that. She was rude, blowing smoke on me, not even offering me a cigarette. I don't smoke, but she didn't know that. Maybe she could sense it. Maybe she noticed that my eyes were watering. Maybe she was just fucking with me and enjoying it. One thing was sure, though: we connected.

Suddenly the smoke was not as clear and beautiful anymore; the sun could not cut through it. I saw that the sky had become less blue, more like dirty water. Gray clouds were starting to gang up together, getting ready for a fight. A big and dirty cotton candy field was taking shape.

I looked at the woman. She continued to smoke. The ducks were leaving, and so were the swans. The worms were crawling back into their holes in the ground. I noticed a dog was trotting around the drunk lying in the grass, licking the bird crap off his face. The man woke up, totally lost. He managed to get up, brush the crap off himself, and lurch away toward the park exit.

The blazer man took his old lady under his arm and strolled off. *Finally,* I thought. Finally it was only her and me. I could focus on her and her beauty. The smoke, the lips. I noticed that the smoke was gone. I turned to look at her and ask if she was done blowing it in my face.

She was gone. Not there. She'd disappeared. Fuck. I needed to see the sun to light her up and make her visible. Powerful thing that sun. We see everything differently in its presence. It brings life to the world.

7

It was Monday morning, and the first quarter of the year was coming to an end. Rain was pouring down from the gray skies like a waterfall. Further east toward the bay, I could see clear skies and the hope for sun. I was standing outside the door of my apartment building, taking shelter underneath the small roof just above the door. The taxi I'd ordered to take me to the airport was late. Every time it showered, it was like it was the first time. All the drivers suddenly lost their ability to drive and started to behave like student drivers, terrified by their instructor and the possibility of failure.

My phone vibrated in my pocket, and I hoped it was the driver texting me that he was just around the corner. To my disappointment, it was Hank sending me a message about how excited he was for the trip and that he'd just packed his silver flask. We were catching a flight bound for Las Vegas and SHOW's annual global sales conference. This year, nine thousand employees were being flown from all around the globe to the city where you could do whatever, whenever. SHOW had chartered planes for everyone, and we would all fly together, flight after flight, taking over the skies, conquering Las Vegas, and leaving as winners.

I was excited, although I didn't know what to expect. I wondered if I would run into Maggie. I wondered if she had fucked the guy at the nightclub in LA. I wondered what I should say to her if I saw her.

I had told my mother about the trip, and she was almost as excited as I was. She called all her friends weeks in advance, telling them about how amazing it was that I was going to the conference, that everything was provided and paid for, and that we had our own airplanes taking us there.

She said that she'd mentioned it to my father when they talked briefly a couple of weeks earlier, but he wasn't impressed, saying that it was a waste of time, money, and soul. It was ludicrous to pour so much money into the mafia-driven city of the devil, and it was an evil trick of SHOW's to take us there and brainwash us into a cult.

The taxi finally arrived outside my building ten minutes late. I grabbed my bag, ran to the car, and jumped in. The driver said he was sorry but the rain had caused traffic jams because people in California didn't know how to drive in the rain. According to him, California drivers should think of the vets who fought in the rainforests in Vietnam and not complain about a little water falling from the sky.

During the forty-minute trip to the airport, he told me stories from his own Vegas trips, mostly involving prostitutes, cheap drinks, and slot machines. When we arrived at the airport, I told him to add five dollars to the total bill before I paid with my corporate card and asked for the receipt so I could expense the trip. Together with the receipt, he gave me a business card to a strip club in Las Vegas called Crazy Czech Girl. He said I should go there, tell them I knew Frankie from San Francisco, and then wait for a surprise. I smiled politely, thanked him for the ride and the advice, and hurried into the departure hall.

I'd brought only a carry-on bag with me, packed with swimwear, three pairs of underwear, three pairs of black socks, a pair of shorts, one white T-shirt, one black T-shirt, one black button-up shirt, one gray jacket, a pair of sneakers, a box of painkillers, and sunglasses. Because it was a chartered flight, we'd already been provided boarding passes by SHOW the previous week. Since I didn't have to check in, I went straight to the airport bar to meet up with Hank, Gabe, and Daniel. Gabe had been there for an hour already because he always worried while traveling, particularly that he would be late and miss the plane. Hank had arrived just five minutes before and was already drinking a gin and tonic. Gabe was drinking a black coffee. I ordered an orange juice. Hank asked me if anything was wrong, and I said it was too early for me and I'd get a drink on the flight. He stroked his beard and smiled.

Daniel wasn't there, which didn't surprise us. Hank said that if Daniel missed the flight, he'd slap him in the face next time he saw him.

We finished our drinks and strolled to the gate to board the plane. We still hadn't heard anything from Daniel, even though I'd texted him when we left the bar saying he should hurry up.

The plane was an old jumbo jet with three gray leather seats per row on the left and right sides and four seats in the middle. The seating wasn't reserved, so we took seats in a middle section. I sat down in the aisle seat on the left side of our row. Gabe and Hank took the center seats, and Hank saved the seat on his right for Daniel.

"Traf Air–Charter & Cargo" was printed in black on the back of each seat. The flight attendants bustled around trying to get everyone to turn off their phones, tablets, and laptops. Being part of the legendary tech company as we were, it wasn't an easy crowd to convince to put their phones away. Maybe treating us with phones for Christmas hadn't been such a clever idea.

Daniel appeared and took the seat next to Hank, who said that Daniel was lucky he'd made it. Shortly after, the plane took off for Las Vegas. As soon as the fasten seat belt sign went off, the crew pulled out the drink carts, and I ordered a whiskey on the rocks.

8

We got to Las Vegas around eleven o'clock, and the heat that hit me after we exited the arrivals terminal made me sweat a bit as we trudged to the chartered buses that would take us to the hotels. Our bus was headed toward the Bellagio.

When we arrived at the hotel, I checked in and got the key to my suite. Beautiful women paraded around in dresses and high heels, and guys wearing suits and big smiles tagged behind.

I said bye to the guys, ambled over to the row of elevators by the front desk, and pressed the button. The doors opened immediately, and I stepped through. I pushed number twenty-nine, and after a smooth ride, I ventured out and found my room. I put the key card in the door and heard a click and the door opened. The feeling that anything was possible hit me as soon as I saw the view of Las Vegas through the room's full-length windows.

I opened the minibar, where the baby bottles of liquor were perfectly lined up by category: vodka on the top shelf, whiskey on the second, gin on the third. A liquid candy store for adults. I took out two baby vodkas and a can of Red Bull, poured it all into a glass, set it on the sofa table, and took off my clothes. I went to the bathroom, splashed water on my face, and stared into the mirror while the water dripped down into the sink. Orchids stood next to the sink, and the smell took me back to childhood and the trips to visit my father in New York. Orchids were my mother's favorite flower. She always bought them for my father when she visited him, but because his job consumed his attention, he was not able to take care of them, and they always died a slow death. I hated it. It was to make up for the dead flowers that my father took me to the botanical garden whenever I visited.

The water had stopped dripping off my face, and I took the white robe hanging in the bathroom and put it on. It was made of cotton and smelled like lavender. I padded back to the living room area, took a seat on the big black couch, turned on the television, and took a sip of my drink while a line on the screen appeared:

Welcome to Las Vegas and the Bellagio, Mr. Janoski.

I looked out the window. "Welcome to Las Vegas, Mr. Janoski," I said aloud to myself. The show had started.

9

It was a clear night. The stars were shining in the sky over the Nevada desert and the Las Vegas Strip. The guys and I stood by the bar at the welcome party that was being held by the pool at the Bellagio. SHOW had reserved the entire area for the private party, and there were trays of food, drinks, and DJs. The liquor was flowing, legs were dancing, and the laughs were piling up.

Daniel could barely focus; his head was spinning around like a tank turret aiming for its target. I couldn't blame him. All the women were beautiful, wearing high heels and dresses. My head was also spinning, but for a different reason—Maggie. I saw the predator Ryan stalking around like a hit man in a suit with a glass of orange juice in his hand. I hoped he would walk straight into one of the swimming pools.

Hank said that the DJ was shit and that he couldn't listen to the horrible house mixes much longer. He finished his drink and told us he'd be right back, then waded into the crowd. Once Hank disappeared, I looked around and saw Maggie standing on the other side of the large pool. She wore a black dress with a slit up the leg on one side.

I could barely breathe. I felt like I was going to throw up. The feeling got worse when I saw who she was talking to. Ryan had found her. My heart rate increased, and my brain didn't know what to do. Usually my rationality didn't give up on me, but now it vanished. I knew I had to leave while I still had some of it left in my brain.

10

The bartender had on a white shirt and a black bow tie. He looked high, his face lacking expression while he mixed our margaritas. We'd left the SHOW party and were sitting in a bar on the casino floor. A man I recognized from the office sat on the other side of the bar with a drink in his hand. There were four empty glasses in front of him next to an open package of Marlboro cigarettes. A blond woman sat on his left and a brunette on his right. Both of them were flirting with him, and he didn't know who to focus on. His eyes went back and forth between the two of them, making him seem nervous. The two women both had voluptuous breasts enhanced by excellent cleavage. The man was talking, and they were responding with fake laughs to everything he said and stroking him on his neck and back every now and then. I wondered whether he knew they were prostitutes or if he didn't care. The battle continued for a while, but by the time we were done with our first margarita, the man decided to go with the blond and left the brunette sitting alone at the bar. Before we got our second round of drinks, she was sitting with a new guy, laughing at his jokes, stroking him on his back, pretending to listen. Maybe she liked it. Maybe it got her excited and turned on. Maybe not.

The margaritas kept coming. Hank was still gone, and Gabe started to get drunk. He began to lose control over his movements, and his body was like a marionette in action. Daniel had a constant smile on his face, flashing it at every woman who passed.

A bunch of people from our office wandered by, including Nicky. They were on their way to XS, a club with an outdoor pool area at Wynn Encore casino. We decided to join them. We chugged our margaritas and took a limousine to XS. The champagne bottles were popping around the pool area under the stars, the music was loud, and the crowds were dancing. We had a huge table with bottle service and a view of the dance floor reserved for us by the pool. Nicky didn't notice the water and tumbled right into it, which resulted in an unexpected bath for her and then some entertainment for the rest of us when she climbed out in her wet dress.

At around two, Gabe left the party, saying he was drunk and going home to his girlfriend. I wished him luck and hoped he'd realize when he got out of the club that he was in Las Vegas and not home in San Francisco.

Two women in their forties approached me and Daniel on the dance floor, and we circled up like in a courtship ritual. After a while, it was settled who wanted whom; the tall red-haired woman locked on to me, and the shorter brunette decided to go for Daniel. We split up and were now dancing in pairs. It was sweaty, wild, and intense. Every now and then, Maggie popped up in my mind, and I looked around for her. I hoped that she wouldn't see me with this woman; on the other hand, I had no obligation to Maggie, so I got angry with myself for even caring.

The heat, dancing, and liquor started to have an impact, and my mouth became dry. I said I was going to the bar for a drink, and the redhead followed me, as did Daniel and the brunette. The brunette wanted to go gamble, to which we all agreed, and we immediately left the club for the casino floor at the Palazzo. There we sat down by a roulette table. The casino was almost empty. It must have been late night, or early morning, or both. The redhead opened her purse and pulled out a couple of hundred-dollar bills.

She gave three of them to me and told me to play. I said I had my own money, but she insisted she wanted to take care of me. Daniel got some hundred-dollar bills from the brunette as well. His smile was priceless.

The waiter came, and I ordered four rum and Cokes, then quickly changed my mind and made it eight. I put a hundred dollars on red twenty-one, and forty seconds later I was a hundred dollars poorer.

The redhead asked us what we were doing in Vegas, and I said we were at a conference. The brunette said that they were too and asked which company we worked for. I said it was a tech company, and the redhead asked if it was SHOW. She smiled and put her hand on my thigh under the table. Daniel started to laugh, and the brunette said that they also worked at SHOW, as did many of the guests partying at XS that night.

The brunette woman was insanely drunk and kept trying to put her hands on the roulette wheel to give it a spin. The croupier was getting annoyed and told her several times to behave or leave the table. She didn't listen, and after a couple of complaints, she told him that he should stop acting like her husband. Daniel asked if she was married, and she said she was but that she took off her ring when she partied because she wanted some fun, and her husband was a bore who only liked to watch football and drink beer with his friends.

The redhead said her husband was also a fucking bore who never surprised her, just sat at home watching the television, hoping to get a blow job. She added that he never did, but he wouldn't give up. Sometimes he'd even ask for one with a desperate look on his face.

In the middle of the two women whining about their husbands, I suddenly heard the sound of a slow clap approaching from behind. It ended with a hard slap on my back. It was Alex: drunk, alone. He asked me if he could borrow three hundred dollars because he'd just made a deal with a guy behind the slot machines to buy some cocaine. He'd lost both his own credit card and the company credit card and was out of cash. I told him I'd just spent all my cash and asked him why he was barefoot. He said he'd given his shoes away to a bum outside a strip club in exchange for a cigarette. He claimed that Hank had smoked all of his in the club and then snatched the Marlboro pack that Alex had just bought. I asked him where Hank was, and Alex started to talk about a strip club called Crazy Czech Girl, a Chinese guy, and a taxi driver with a shotgun. Nothing he said made sense, and I was too drunk to figure it out.

A security guard came and stood by the table. Alex stared at him for a couple of seconds before he turned around and crept away, shoeless.

"Excuse me, miss, I'm afraid we can't let you play any longer. Please step away from the table," the security guy told the brunette.

"Fucking loser. You're not my husband," she said.

"I'm going to ask you to step away one more time. You're too intoxicated to gamble."

"Fuck you, I'm independent. Do you know where I work? At fucking SHOW!"

"I don't care," he said. "This is your last chance to step away, or I will have to remove you and put you in a holding room."

The redhead told her friend to get her shit together and listen to the guard. The brunette took her heels off, grabbed her purse, then turned around and said that she was leaving this crappy table because the service was horrible. She took Daniel by his shirt, kissed him, and stomped off, leaving the heels behind like Cinderella. The redhead gripped my neck, kissed me, and went after her friend.

We watched them totter away across the almost empty casino floor. Some old women were sitting by the slot machines; for them it was morning and a new day of gambling, hope, and misery. For us, it was bedtime before a new day of hangovers and SHOW conference seminars.

11

The sun was shining in through the giant windows of my suite. It hadn't crossed my mind to close the curtains when I got back from the casino, and now I was being punished by the sharp light drilling through my eyelids and into my pounding brain. My whole body shook. I could barely lie still and couldn't decide if it was less painful to lie on my stomach, side, or back. I opened my right eye and tried to look at the clock standing on the night table next to the bed, but I couldn't see the time. Last night's drinks had stolen my eye's ability to perform well enough on its own, and it was too painful to keep them both open. I closed the right eye, waited for a minute, then opened the left one. This time I managed to see the time. It was 9:38 a.m. The conference opening seminar started at ten.

I tried to get up and failed. I tried again, failed again. Every time I tried to get out of the bed, my head didn't go with my body or my body didn't go with my head. I was broken in all possible ways. I needed to find another way. I threw some pillows down on the floor by the side of the bed. Then, I slowly rolled out of the bed and fell onto them.

Crawling on the floor toward the sofa table where the remote to the curtains lay, I felt ashamed of myself. I reached the remote and pressed all the buttons until one of them closed the curtains and the room became dark. The sun would no longer bother me as I recovered. I dragged myself up onto the sofa next to the table and reached for a bottle of water. I forced my arm toward my mouth. My hands and head were trembling, and I spilled on my chest while I drank. I thought of Mr. Gibbons and his shakes.

Maybe I could blame the redhead who gave me money and drank with me or maybe her husband for being an asshole to his wife, making it so she needed some excitement with me. But I couldn't complain. This was my fault entirely. I couldn't blame anyone but myself for this fucking hangover.

The more I looked around the room for my painkillers, the more the amusement park in my head grew, spinning around in all directions at once. When I couldn't see the pills anywhere, I assumed they must be in the bathroom. I had to get up from the sofa, cross the living room, pass the bed, and find my way into the bathroom. It felt like a cruel mission, but I had to do it. I put my left foot down on the floor, pushed myself out with my right foot, and rolled over and down on the floor with my hands out to mitigate the fall. Once I was on my hands and knees, I started my journey, moving like a tired old dog.

When I finally made it, I grabbed the sink and pulled myself up to a standing position. I saw my pants lying on the floor. I pushed them out of the bathroom with my foot, grabbed the painkillers lying next to my toothbrush on the sink, swallowed two of them, and lurched out, kicking my slacks toward the bed. Once there, I sat, leaned over to pick them up, and then lay down. I managed to pull the pants on after some struggle.

I found a white T-shirt on the bed, put it on, and searched for my shoes. I couldn't find them. I took another pair out of my bag, staggered out of the room, and slammed the door behind me.

* * *

I arrived at the conference center twenty minutes late. The massive main hall was filled with SHOW employees from all around the globe, nine thousand of us. Everyone was waiting for our CEO, Tim Nelson, to come to the stage and welcome us. I saw that I was not the only one feeling like I'd been run over by a train that morning. The posture of many made them look like they would fall off their chairs any second. I saw an empty chair next to a guy with glasses and a ponytail, and I took a seat. The guy noticed me and nodded. I nodded back. Two or three minutes later, Tim Nelson showed up in New Balance sneakers and a black hoodie. The employees in the hundreds of rows stood up from their chairs, cheering and applauding. Nine thousand people standing up and clapping—I had never seen anything like it. It could have been God onstage. It was impressive, awe inspiring, and at the same time scary as hell. I didn't know if I belonged to a new technology cult or if I was at a rock concert.

The noise of the crowd made my headache even worse. After some welcoming words, Nelson stepped down, and a yoga master came onstage. She asked everyone to follow her lead, and a nine-thousand-person yoga group was born. I stood up, felt like vomiting, and left. I ran to the closest bathroom, locked myself into a stall, sat on my knees, and threw up into the toilet. The pain from my head diminished, as though it had trailed down into the toilet and then the sewer system.

I went back to my room and fell asleep.

12

"Fucking amateur." Hank laughed.

Hank, Daniel, Gabe, and I were sitting at a table in a restaurant inside Caesars Palace having dinner. Hank told us about Alex, whom he'd seen in a strip club the previous night sitting in a corner, smoking cigarettes with a stripper. Hank had walked over to him to say hi and bum some smokes. He noticed that Alex's mouth was wet and that he had some white liquid above his upper lip. Alex asked Hank if he'd ever tried breast milk before. The stripper he was sitting with had apparently given birth two weeks before, and Alex was sucking breast milk from her between drags on his cigarette.

Alex had told Hank that he was out of cash and all his credit cards were gone. He'd asked a prostitute for a blow job at the Bellagio and didn't have enough cash to pay for it, so he'd given her his credit cards instead.

My hangover was almost gone. The rib-eye steak I was eating for dinner had helped me to recover. After throwing up that morning, I'd slunk back to my room and slept the rest of the day, missing out on all the company seminars presenting the future of SHOW. I promised myself not to party again so I wouldn't miss the presentations the second day.

My will let me down as soon as Hank ordered a third round of Jameson and ginger ale. We drank, partied, and gambled until the next morning. We didn't go to the conference the next day either, except for Gabe, who was there on time. He'd heard stories about people getting fired, which put him on his best behavior.

In fact, two guys were fired for demolishing a suite, one woman for passing out by the front desk in the lobby, and some others for sexually harassing coworkers. Luckily no one in our group was accused of anything. Even Alex had made it through so far.

On the third night, SHOW had arranged a private concert with Justin Timberlake at the Sam Boyd Stadium, and all of the bars and restaurants served drinks and food free of charge.

After the concert, we ended up at a party in a hotel suite at the Bellagio with around fifty people, many from SHOW. Three women were sitting on the floor next to the sofa massaging each other's feet while talking about a Chinese massage therapist named Mr. Pung who was supposed to solve all their problems. One girl said he was magical and prodded the other two to go to him when they were back home in London. She said that his hands would solve all their mental issues as well as their physical ones. Mr. Pung apparently knew which nerves to push to affect both mind and body in a pleasant way.

Hank asked them if there was a Mrs. Pung who performed similar services, and they said that there was no Mrs. Pung, but that he should go to the Strip if he was looking for treatment. He said he'd already been to a strip club twice during the three-day conference and that he wasn't interested in prostitutes. He'd rather stay at the party and watch the women massage each other.

A guy was doing coke on the coffee table with a black straw, three lines at a go. The guy next to him was snorting pepper; he was out of coke but got a rush just from sniffing things up. He started to bleed when the pepper burned through the inside of his nose. Every time the cokehead finished another three lines, he stared at the ceiling and yelled, "I am from fucking SHOW, bitches!"

Watching this, my world instantly stopped, and John's smile popped into my mind. I lost track of everything else going on in that hotel room and fell deeper and deeper into darkness. Miserable things took over my mind: John's cocaine-induced death, Chris's father's cancer, my pop-up store–type relationship with my father, and my secret love for Maggie.

Suddenly I felt something on my face that interrupted my thoughts. It was cold and sticky. The cocaine-snorting loser was shaking a champagne bottle from the minibar and spraying it all over the room. His white coke mustache made him look like an evil Charlie Chaplin. I called him a fucking idiot and left.

I returned to my room and called room service while I threw all my stuff into my bag. My plane back to San Francisco was due to depart in five hours.

My cheeseburger, fries, and vanilla shake were brought to my room by a short Asian guy in glasses. I tipped him ten dollars and wished him well. I ate my burger, drank my shake, thought of Maggie, and fought the anxious thought that my wake-up call would come in just two and a half hours. I was already afraid of the looming hangover; the fear took me by my throat and slowly choked me to sleep.

PART 3

1

I sat at my desk scrolling through my e-mail in-box, which was filled with questions from my clients. I hadn't checked it since we'd left for the conference the previous week. As I browsed through the e-mails, I saw one from Angela at Redlight Pictures. She was wondering if we could have a meeting to discuss and evaluate their marketing strategy. They weren't satisfied, because it had cost them more than it gave in return in the form of sales: our promised numbers didn't make sense.

I didn't respond. I didn't care. It wasn't important. It was just money—fictitious figures on a screen that didn't improve the world in any way. Yet everyone was so obsessed with those figures. No wonder things hadn't gone as we'd promised. Sometimes making things up worked; sometimes it didn't. The clients couldn't do anything about it and just had to trust us. Nobody ever questioned our promises. We were SHOW.

Day in and day out, I pitched solutions to my clients and guaranteed them success for their businesses, telling them it was their time to shine and reap money. I was starting to lose motivation and rarely saw the meaning of it anymore. In the beginning, I had been excited about it. I had been passionate about each one of my clients, their needs, and their goals. Now I felt like a messenger, a

machine telling the same thing to all of them, telling them what
SHOW wanted me to tell them.

I felt nauseated and confused. I left my desk and went to the
bathroom, giving everyone I passed a fake smile, pretending I felt
great. I entered one of the stalls and locked the door behind me,
then vomited into the toilet. It felt relaxing, like a full body massage. I flushed, washed my hands, and left the office. I needed to get
out, breathe fresh air—air that was not contaminated by money,
drugs, and the constant chase for more.

Once outside, I called Chris. He picked up and said he couldn't
talk for long since he was driving and on his way to band practice.

"I met my dad for lunch, and we even scheduled another for
next week," Chris said.

"Glad to hear it," I said.

"Stay Classy has a huge gig in Hollywood coming up before
Memorial Day, at the Viper Room."

"Wow, that's awesome. I'm flying down for that one."

"Nice. It's gonna be great! Listen I have to go. Take care, man."
Chris hung up.

I went to Pacific Heights to relax and enjoy the view from Alta
Plaza Park. From there, I could see the bay. White sailboats cruised
back and forth in the wind. It felt like the world was flat, that it was
never ending, that I could take a leap down Pierce Street, jump
into one of the boats, and take Maggie with me and sail away on
the flatness into eternity without ever coming back.

2

The light breeze moved the palm leaves slowly up and down, side to side, and in circles. Summer was about to start. It was the weekend before Memorial Day, and Los Angeles grew warmer in May. I was standing outside the airport terminal waiting for Chris to pick me up.

We drove straight to Rose Café in Venice, listening to Elton John without saying a word. Chris left the car with the valet, and we went inside. We were instantly offered a table outside, and before we sat down I ordered two mimosas and a full stack of pancakes to share. I asked the waiter to keep the mimosas coming. Later, Chris ordered an omelet, and I ordered huevos rancheros as usual.

"How's your dad?" I asked.

Chris took a big sip of the mimosa, emptying the glass. "Well, meeting up was scary at first. I didn't know what to say, how to react. Hadn't seen him in so many years. He looked so thin and tired," Chris said.

The waiter came in with two fresh mimosas. Then the omelet and my huevos were brought to our table by a different, older waitress a few seconds later.

"He told me he has lung cancer. He said he regrets everything: that he left us, that we lost touch, that our relationship was fucked up. He's sorry he didn't support my music dreams. He was so overtaken by his job and the pleasures that came with it: you know, the parties, money, drinking, women—younger women who wanted something he could offer, who he could exploit because of that."

Chris took a couple of big sips of the new mimosa before he continued. "The funny thing is, Vic, when bad health hits you, you can't protect yourself. No matter how rich you are, how well connected you are, how much power you have—you're just as fucked. There's no getting around that."

He took his sunglasses off and looked at me. "But you know where the difference lies, Vic, between losing yourself to your career or being with your family? When you get sick and thin, you can't keep up with the business and lifestyle, and you're out, alone. Suddenly you have nothing to trade, and they see you as a useless piece of shit. There's no need for you if you can't do your work.

"But your family, those are the ones who care, always. No matter what. That's the difference. And that's when you get desperate and crawl back and regret that you picked the other side. You come back for mercy, just like my father. And we accept you."

We finished our food and drinks and then walked out toward the valet. We picked up the car, tipped the valet guy ten dollars, and drove away.

3

Chris drove me home to my mother's. This time, I wouldn't see Mr. Gibbons sitting alone in his window. I wouldn't be able to go over to his house for a drink like I had at Christmas. I wished I could. My mother had mentioned on the phone when we talked that morning that Mr. Gibbons had passed away two weeks before from Parkinson's disease.

I felt sorry that I hadn't gotten to know him before. Through all these years, I had talked to him only that one Christmas over drinks. I had thought that the old man would sit in the window and stare resentfully forever.

As usual, my mother was ecstatic I was home to visit. She put her homemade meat loaf on my plate for dinner and watched me while I ate it as she asked dozens of questions about everything.

We talked about my sister, Emma. She'd finally stayed single for a couple of months instead of jumping on the first dating train that slowed down to pick her up. We talked about Chris and his dad, the misery that they both suffered. I told her about the conference in Vegas but decided to leave out the parts with the drugs, excessive drinking, and strip clubs.

When I finished the meat loaf, I took a taxi to Hollywood, where I met up with friends for drinks at a bar before Chris's gig at the Viper Room on Sunset Strip.

"Hey, Mr. SHOW! What's happening in the mighty tech world?" our high school friend James said as I strode into the bar.

"Making tons of money, knowing what you browse online, and taking over the world. Besides that, not much," I answered with a grin.

James had a date with him, a short brunette dressed in brown leather boots and a black dress. When she heard that I work at SHOW, her eyes opened up wide and her eyebrows almost shot up to the ceiling. I knew what was coming. I had met people like her before. People who can't believe they're meeting a person from SHOW, that people from SHOW actually exist. They ask all the usual questions about the myths and legends of the almighty company. Most of the time, it meant answering whether it was true that we had a swimming pool in the office, that we had free food and snacks all the time, or that we work only half the day and then play video games and Ping-Pong the rest of the time.

James's date started to ask me everything, asking questions faster than she could listen to my answers. After a couple of minutes, I said I needed to use the restroom. Instead, I went to the bar to order a whiskey from the tattooed bartender girl. I preferred to listen to the drunks in the bar than to James's date's constant barrage of questions.

I should have told her I was a drug dealer. Maybe that would have shut her up. Although, worst-case scenario, that could have made her even more interested considering how stoned she looked. I wished Maggie were there. She wouldn't annoy me like James's date; she would make me smile.

James's date had a tall blond friend with her, and she floated over to me and asked if I had some coke. She stared at me while she sipped a martini. I stared back at her.

"Do I look like a coke dealer?" I asked her.

"Yeah. You do," she said. I didn't do coke but was often mistaken for a coke sniffer by people I met, especially women. I hadn't figured out why.

"Well, thank you, lady. I'm honored. But I'm not."

"You look like a coke dealer who wants to do coke off my mouth and then fuck me in the bathroom. Standing up."

"I'm honored again. And you look like a cokehead that wants to get fucked wherever and whenever for some blow."

She gently took the olive out of her martini, put it in her mouth, and swallowed it. Then she threw her drink in my face. I licked my lips.

James came running over and asked what happened. I told him she'd gotten a bit annoyed that I didn't have any cocaine to offer. And that I didn't want to fuck her in the bathroom. Standing up.

The lights went off and the music stopped. Darkness and silence followed. For a moment, I hoped that John would come back to us from heaven and join Chris's gig. I wondered if this was what it felt like to be dead. Darkness, silence, and eternity. Nothing. It's too hard to imagine nothing. The lights onstage came on, Chris's band came out, and the performance started.

Dreams, hopes, and the future were onstage. The entire club came to life and began jumping around. It immediately killed my musing about there being only darkness and silence on the other side. Now I was sure that there wasn't. The dead were among us, enjoying what we enjoy, together with us in our minds. I pretended John was there, and he had the time of his life.

4

I met Chris on the Venice Beach Boardwalk the next day. It was a hot Sunday afternoon, and we bought two vanilla ice cream cones, then rambled along the boardwalk among the skaters, singers, painters, and dancers. They were all chasing fantasies, unique ones for each of them. I knew none of them were famous, rich, or admired by the world. They were poor, and some were even homeless. Most saw these people as failed artists. Many thought of them as freaks with broken dreams who didn't know how to accept failure, how to give up hope.

The smell of Venice Beach was extraordinary: the mixed scent of pizza, sweat, weed, and the sea made it impossible not to imagine, impossible not to believe. Adding to that was the sound of music, laughter, cheering, and swearing, making it even more difficult not to. All the characters, all the skills and experience, all the hope—everything in its place. It was a creative volcano that could erupt any second.

Hanging out there, I felt like a nobody. I felt like a failure, sitting at my corporate desk every day, working like a robot. My ice cream started to melt in the heat and drip onto my hand. I licked it up. It tasted salty: the breeze from the ocean had even salted the people. It was like the sea was going to eat us all one day and had sent the wind to salt us first.

I told Chris how happy they all looked, the freaks. Happier than most people.

I admired them for chasing their dreams and for not losing hope. Hope is the last thing that leaves your body, and you should hold on to it as long as possible.

I admitted to Chris that I was starting to get tired of my high-end rock star life in the tech world. The benefits, the parties, the money; I couldn't find the meaning of the excess. I couldn't see the meaning of the constant chase for more, the greed that Wall Street had taught us. I wanted to chase dreams instead, my dreams.

The sun began to find its way down toward the horizon. We walked back to the car and turned on the radio. Chris drove me to the airport for my evening flight back to San Francisco. As usual, we didn't speak. The music, the thousands of red and white car lights, and the moment were all that was needed to say good-bye.

5

I had just finished a morning meeting with a client at the office and was moseying back to my desk when my manager came running toward me looking stressed and paranoid. She needed a success story as soon as possible. She was on her way to a review with the top management so they could see that everything was on track at the end of the quarter. She asked me if I could give her some great numbers. I told her that I'd just come back from a meeting in which the company had agreed to increase their spend with SHOW by 28 percent this quarter—all because of another meeting I'd had with them before Memorial Day when I told them to run a large campaign, which had proved successful.

I was lying. It was total bullshit. Yes, I had just had a meeting, but the numbers were pure imagination. I had learned that that was the way it worked at SHOW. I didn't even think about it anymore. The lies came naturally, and the success stories grew more and more extraordinary. The customers would spend their money anyway, and as long as I took the credit for it, nobody cared. As long as it sounded good, nobody checked. Everyone wanted to report great numbers to their managers to get promoted. It was a chain reaction, step by step, level by level.

I went to the cafeteria on my floor for my regular ten thirty coffee with some of the guys. Eric, the self-elected coffee professional was, as usual, making cappuccinos with milky hearts for some women while telling jokes to make them giggle. Alex was standing next to the espresso machine and preaching that we would never find a job that was this well paid where we could get away with doing so little.

We started to talk about work, complaining about our salaries, the new towels in the gym, and the salmon that had been slightly overcooked at lunch the other day. Gabe was whining that his mind was slowly putrefying in this job, that it should be used for better things than selling ads and making up numbers day after day. It was rare to see Gabe riled up. When he was mad about something, it was pure and solid. His anger was well thought out—there were no spontaneous explosions. He always had facts to support his discontent. We all knew that Gabe's opinion could be trusted, and we agreed with him. He could become a worthy politician if he ran for office. I always told him he would get my vote. Politics are like a scene in which it's sometimes better to listen to the voices in the background than the actors at center stage. Gabe had an exquisite mind but was not much of a leading man.

Daniel stood by the panoramic window in the cafeteria and gazed out toward the bay. Usually he was on fire, energetic and excited, his smile taking over the room. Today, he didn't say much.

"What's up, Daniel? You seem a bit down," I said while waiting for my double espresso.

"Yeah, no, I'm just so fucking sick of this, chasing the stupid sales targets. Having to bring in the cashola," he answered, still gazing out.

"That sucks, but you'll make it. You always do. And you know it."

"Yeah, perhaps. But at the moment I feel like a crackhead collecting cigarette butts off Market Street. Honestly, I would actually prefer that right now."

There were only three weeks left of the sales quarter, and many employees were stressed about their targets. Everyone wanted to perform well and hit personal goals in order to get a nice sales bonus and a good track record to improve the chances of a promotion. Some, like Alex, had already reached their targets and could relax and play video games.

"I like crackheads," Alex said. "They're fun to talk to."

"I have to make some calls," Daniel said and left.

6

I was sitting on the bench in the dressing room, breathing heavily and stretching my legs after my forty-minute morning workout at the office gym. Sweat was dripping off my eyebrows and down to the floor. I had on a brand-new pair of Nikes, which I'd bought two days before when I came out of a bar drunk and passed a Nike store off Union Square. The drinks had filled me with confidence, and when I saw the shoes through the store window, I decided they were the last piece in the puzzle that would help me get a date with Maggie.

I leaned forward and untied the laces, then slowly took the shoes off. It hurt a bit: the blisters on both my heels from the new footwear were not what I had wished for. After a shower, I put on my favorite pair of underwear—black Calvin Klein boxer briefs— and took new socks and a fresh pair of jeans and black shirt from my bag. I put some Davidoff cologne on my neck and combed my hair. Then I put the socks on and looked at myself in the mirror. I smiled at my reflection, wearing only underwear and socks. I put my jeans and shirt on, rolled up the sleeves, and put my watch on my left wrist.

Then, I took a seat on the bench again, packed my stuff, and put my brown boots on before heading to the cafeteria for breakfast.

The workout made me hungry, and I loaded one plate with scrambled eggs and bacon and another with French toast and fresh fruit. I took a seat by the window. It was still early, seven forty-five, and not many people were in yet. It was calm and quiet compared with lunchtime, which was always hectic and chaotic.

After taking one bite, I put down my fork and went over to get a glass of orange juice. Just as I put the glass to the machine where the oranges get squeezed, I heard someone behind me say hi. It was her, Maggie.

"How are you?" she said.

"Oh, I'm good. And you?"

"I'm good. Are you having breakfast?" She looked at the juice machine and smiled just as I felt the juice run over the top of the glass and onto my hand. I released the button.

"Oh, shit," I said, embarrassed.

She laughed.

"Yeah, join me. I'm sitting down by the windows facing Townsend Street," I said.

"Sure, I'll just go grab some fruit and oatmeal."

This was my chance to ask her out. It was time to cowboy the fuck up.

We ate and talked: talked about the Vegas conference, about work, about me, about her, about life. Watching her facial expressions up close just made me want her even more—right there, on the table, with the bacon and eggs.

We were done with our food, and I felt that my chance would be gone soon. I had to act fast.

"Do you like salmon?" I asked.

"Yeah, I love it," she said.

"I'll take you to a great place sometime," I said nervously.

"Sounds nice."

"Maybe in two weeks, once the quarter is over."

"Yeah, why not? I have to go, meeting with my manager. End of quarter reporting, you know. So glad it's done soon! See you around." She left.

7

The sales quarter would be over in two days, and I was sitting at the office with Daniel creating a performance report for my manager, which she needed to present to her manager, who would present it to his manager, and so on. The chain was painfully long. Everyone had a different agenda. We all worked toward our own sales targets and worried only about our own performance. Promotions weren't based on natural selection: the smartest or the most loyal wouldn't necessarily win. The choice was increasingly based on who could adapt to the hypocrisy and manipulate the data into the most beautiful presentation. It was survival of the hypocrites.

The last couple of weeks, I'd noticed that Daniel had lost a bit of himself. He was the most hard-working, smart, and loyal person in our department, but something wasn't right. He didn't care about his clients; he didn't respond to their needs.

"Fuck this report," he said. "These numbers don't help us or the clients in any way. It's just to make someone else higher up look good."

"I know. That's the game, bud. You either have to play it or walk away. It's corporate America," I answered.

"Over the last month, I've been considering leaving this moneymaking factory. I'll tell you a secret, Vic, if you can promise me not to tell the others?"

"I won't," I said.

"Good. You know that we have a couple of shrinks at SHOW, right? That each employee can use. They're in the medical center on the second floor." He gestured toward the floor.

"I know. I'm not a big fan of psychologists."

I thought back to when I was seven and my mother had taken me to a child psychologist in Los Angeles. She thought I needed to talk to someone since my dad didn't live with us. The doctor's name was Derek Schwartz, and apparently he was one of the best child shrinks in the area. I remember sitting on a dark-blue sofa in the small waiting room outside his office while my mother was in the ladies' room. Games and toys lay around on the coffee table in front of me, and I started to play with a deck of cards.

I had counted them over and over again, and my count always ended at fifty. My father had told me a deck should have fifty-two cards. The missing cards made me feel uncomfortable and suspicious. I didn't like when things didn't make sense.

There was an aquarium standing on a shelf on the other side of the room. A goldfish swam around in circles inside it. I left the card deck and went to examine the aquarium more closely. I could see only one fish. Where was the other? Shouldn't there be at least two so that they could play with each other? I figured it was missing: something was wrong, just as with the card deck.

Daniel nodded. "Yeah, I'm not a fan of psychologists either, but I went to sign up for an appointment. I've been feeling low lately, searching for a meaning for what the hell I'm doing here. It feels like I am slowly dying every day, and everything I do is useless. You know what they said when I wanted to sign up for an appointment?"

"That you should do some cocaine and you'll be fine?" I smiled.

"Wouldn't surprise me. No, that there is a waiting list of two thousand employees, and the first available appointment is in eight weeks. Aren't we supposed to work at the best place in the world?

How can there be so many in need of a shrink? It's this chase for sales targets and promotions, man. I'm telling you. It's madness."

"That's fucked," I said. "Shrinks won't solve any issues anyway; only the initiator of the issue can fix it. Or the one exposed to it."

At the shrink's office, my mother hadn't understood about the fish.

"Victor! Don't touch the aquarium—you're scaring the fish," she'd cried when she came back from the ladies' room. She didn't realize that the fish was already scared, being imprisoned all by itself in that horrible little waiting room with kids staring at it all day.

At that moment, the big brown wooden door to Dr. Schwartz's office had opened. I was expecting a tall man in a white jacket with a friendly look, like the doctors I'd seen on TV, but out came a short man with round glasses and a red shirt tucked into a pair of khaki pants. I could see the reflection of the ceiling light on his bald head. He had a gold tooth, and it glimmered as he smiled. He introduced himself and welcomed us inside the office. My mother walked in, but I refused. I told them both I had nothing to say and that I needed to count the card deck again. After some debate, my mother decided she would go talk with Dr. Schwartz by herself since the appointment was already paid for anyway.

Ten years later, I saw a headline in the *LA Times*, "Famous child psychologist Schwartz convicted of child molesting."

8

She giggled when I told her how grizzly bears catch their fish breakfast during the September salmon run. I was sitting with Maggie at my favorite spot in Pacific Heights, where Alta Plaza Park meets Pierce and Jackson. When I'd bought the two salmon and goat cheese sandwiches from The Grove down at Fillmore Street, I'd been seized by an irrational fear that Maggie was allergic to fish, even though she had told me that she loved salmon.

The July sun, the view of the bay and the boats, and the silence all combined to create a picture-perfect moment. Now and then as we talked, she came out of her shell and became herself, not just an office employee. Her secret inside was visible for a few seconds that day.

We sat there overlooking the bay, eating our sandwiches and talking for two hours. Then we said we should do it again and hugged good-bye. She ambled down Pierce Street toward the marina with the sailing boats in the background. I stayed and watched until she was gone.

I still hadn't figured out how she'd managed to tear my wall down.

9

"Fuck, that's good," Hank whispered as he sipped his whiskey.

We had just ordered drinks at the Rickhouse and had three full whiskey glasses on the counter in front of us. Daniel said he was buying all night: the camel trading had been extremely lucrative during the summer months, and he wanted to celebrate. Hank said that that was great and told the bartender to keep the whiskey coming.

It was Saturday night, and the place was crowded. We were filling up before heading to a housewarming party in Noe Valley. Our colleague Anna had moved in with her boyfriend, who had recently finished an interior design degree. They wanted to show what a great job he had done with the place. Hank said it would probably look like shit because people with degrees lack talent, and design isn't something you can just learn in school: you need passion.

Daniel said he'd heard that the pickup-school guys were planning to use this party as a testing field for their newest students. I wondered what school and students Daniel was talking about, and he started to laugh at me.

"They're like the drug lords," said Daniel, "but instead of drugs they sell classes in how to pick up women. A lot of the software engineers at work go to their seminars."

"So guys are paying these two to teach them how to pick up girls? Then they take them to parties to practice?" I asked.

"Exactly. Beautiful, isn't it?" Daniel smiled.

"So, how often do you go there, Daniel?" Hank asked with a grin.

"I went once just for fun to see what it was. It was horrible. They were talking about the importance of dressing up like a fucking circus clown. Apparently that will do it to get a girl."

"Idiots. They don't know shit," Hank muttered and finished his whiskey.

He looked at the bartender and pointed his finger at the empty glass. The bartender nodded.

"How about that Ryan guy, with the data sheets and algorithms? Is he involved in it as well?" I said.

"Nah, he's too clever for them. They're just running a bullshit show. Ryan is going deep data mining on that shit, and only for himself," Daniel said. "He told me a story about a girl from work that he had been flirting with for a while. He had been working and collecting data for two or three months, trying everything. Eventually he managed to invite himself to her place to help her install a new TV. She'd told him a couple weeks earlier that she was thinking of buying a new TV, and obviously he noted that down and was prepared for the next time he met her. In some magical way, he managed to fuck her on the living room floor."

"My balls would enjoy that," Hank said.

"Yeah, that guy is crazy," Daniel said.

We finished our drinks, paid the tab, left a twenty on the bar, and ventured out into the darkness. We hailed a cab that drove us to Noe Valley and the party.

I could hear the music from the party all the way down to the street. The balcony of their apartment was filled with people smoking. I could smell weed; it was so strong that I felt a bit high myself.

We made our way inside the building and up the stairs to the fourth floor. The door to the apartment was open, and as we walked in, we were immediately greeted by Anna. She had vodka in one hand and champagne in the other. She was wearing a white dress that showed major cleavage and black high heels. I liked what I saw. She never dressed up at the office.

"Told you it would look like shit," Hank whispered in my ear.

Hank was right. He was often right. Maybe too often for his own ego. The place wasn't horrible, but it definitely didn't look like an interior designer had been inside. The apartment was gray, the shades didn't match, and the furniture was not arranged in a practical way. The living room door couldn't even be fully opened because it hit the white sofa that stood right at the entrance to the room. Maybe it was done to create some great effect, but I never saw whatever it was. Maybe we didn't understand his talent.

Daniel pointed out the two guys running the pickup school. They weren't hard to spot: one was wearing red pants, a blue shirt, and green sunglasses, and the other was also colorfully dressed, just in different hues. Together, they reminded me of some parrots I'd seen at the San Francisco Zoo the year before.

Nicky was at the party but didn't seem stoned. She told me that she was taking it easy because she'd been partying too much lately and needed a break. Work had been stressful toward the end of the sales quarter, and she'd taken some crazy business trips to LA the last few weeks to boost her sales performance.

She nodded at the pickup-school guys like she knew them. They ignored her.

"Nice guys," I said.

"Nah, bunch of douche bags. They refer to themselves as pickup artists." She laughed. "You remember my friend Maggie, who you met at the airport on the way down to LA?"

"Maggie? Yeah, I do. The brunette," I said like I didn't care.

"Exactly. One of those fucking pickup artists managed to trick her into going to bed."

My blood pressure went up, and my heart rate increased. I felt like throwing up right there, right on Nicky's breasts. A fucking pickup artist had fucked Maggie.

"He's a cokehead. I fucking hate him," Nicky continued. "He was hitting on Chloe at work the week after when Maggie was standing next to her."

"What a douche bag—she deserves someone better. Listen, I have to go. Enjoy your night, Nicky."

I couldn't stay. I didn't want to watch that cokehead slouching around like a sleazy fucking pimp whispering fake bullshit into drunk women's ears.

Anger grew inside me, but I couldn't blame Maggie. I'd fucked other people too. Obviously we didn't have any obligation to each other. Yet something was chewing at my brain and heart.

10

Sitting at my desk on a rainy Monday morning, I couldn't get Maggie out of my mind.

Work was rough. Everyone was cheating the system, cheating their colleagues, cheating their managers. The constant chase for better numbers and performance scores made me start doing it as well. I began to slack on the job, skipping work and lying to my clients and managers. I didn't give a dusty fuck. I felt chained, like in a factory. I felt like a dog under total control, doing what the owner said so I didn't miss out on food.

Alex came by, wondering if I wanted to go play video games with him. I told him I wasn't in the mood. He asked me how that was possible and if I'd really rather sit and do my meaningless work. I said I was sick of my job and would rather get a drink than play games.

He stared down at me and then took a chair that was standing behind me and pulled it up to my desk.

"You know what I hate the most in this world? Do you?" Alex demanded.

"No, tell me."

He leaned back in the chair and put his feet on my desk. His white sneakers were dirty and smelled like rubber and cheese. The shoelaces were untied and looked like tiny white snakes on the desk.

"I'll tell you, Vic. The thing I hate the most in this world is people. Fucking people. Humans, they're disgusting. I can't stand them. They're idiots, lunatics, and hypocrites. There're two different kinds of people in this world: barbarians and conservators. That's it. They're both disgusting in their own way."

He leaned forward and grabbed the can of Coke sitting on my desk. He leaned back and looked around carefully. When he opened it, the sparkling bubbles of the Coke sounded fresh and alive. Quickly, he took some big sips. With his other hand, he pulled a silver flask from his pocket, opened it, and poured some of its contents into the can.

"The barbarians are the ones destroying this world, changing it to suit them better, to give themselves power and money. In their world, the root of evil is the conservators. The conservators, on the other hand, want to keep the world as it is and work against change and innovation. They want to keep the world the same because it suits them. They're afraid that change will take their power and money away. In the conservators' world, the root of evil is the barbarians." Alex took some sips from the can. "And then, my friend, we have a war. Neither of them is the root of all evil: the root of all evil is money."

Alex poured some more from the flask into the can. "You and me, we are barbarians. We are fighting in the corporate war, the market-share war."

"I know, we're soldiers," I said. "Soldiers in an army that have to perform and execute our tasks, together as a team, as a company."

"Fuck no. Don't worry too much about it. Not our circus, not our monkeys." He passed me the can and gave me an insistent look. Five seconds later, I was drinking rum and Coke at my desk at ten o'clock in the morning.

11

Nicky had been offered a marketing position at the New York office, and she was hosting a good-bye party at Rickhouse the night before her last day. The bar was crowded. Everyone liked Nicky.

I was there with Hank, Daniel, Gabe, and Alex. The drug lords were there, as were the pickup artists. Ryan was strutting around searching for prospects. Eric was watching yet another colleague leave while he was still stuck in the same job.

Chloe stood at the bar next to Nicky. She was looking at me, and I waved to her and then turned back to the guys. Daniel smiled and said she still wanted me; she wanted to use me to make her ex jealous and satisfy his fetish for other guys having sex with her. I told him that would never happen again.

My nerves were shaky that evening. I was wondering if Maggie would show up and if she would kiss the pickup artist in front of me. Nicky turned around and saw us. I motioned for her to come over to our table.

"Hey, Nicky, congrats on the new gig," said Alex. "So you're going over to New York to build up a new Wall Street. It's modern trading. Stockbrokers are old. Ad brokers are the new kings."

"Thanks, yeah, sure. I'll be the female ad wolf."

"Sounds sexy. Give me a hug. I'll miss those tits of yours."

Alex hugged her hard. Nicky laughed and called him a creep. She saw Maggie coming in on the other side of the bar and ran over to hug her.

I sat in silence, staring at Maggie just as I had the first time I saw her. I couldn't stop. She looked our way, met my eyes, and smiled. Everyone has a smile, but hers was something more. Hers was the kind you wanted to wake up to in the morning, the kind you wanted to see when you drank your coffee and when you came home at night.

The douche bag that Nicky said had manipulated Maggie into bed closed in on her. It was disgusting to watch. I turned around.

A moment later, Chloe approached me. She was tipsy already, saying she couldn't stand those losers from the pickup school anymore. They'd told her they were just there to fuck, not to say goodbye to Nicky. We went to the bar for a drink, and one became two and then three. Chloe could handle a lot of liquor, more than most women.

People were slowly leaving. It was Wednesday and almost midnight. I went to the restroom and bumped into Hank.

"There you are. How's it going with Chloe?" he asked.

"We're just talking and drinking. Where are the others?"

"Sure you are. Gabe obviously went home. Daniel is drunk as fuck and chatting with the bar lady. She's been serving him gin and tonics without the gin for the last thirty minutes, but he's too wasted to notice." Hank washed his hands in the sink.

"What an idiot." I laughed.

"Nicky just bought some weed from the drug lords. I'm going home with her now to smoke."

"Really? Her last night in SF. Why go with her tonight?"

"I guess you'll never know. By the way, that Maggie chick just left with one of the pickup assholes." Hank walked out of the bathroom.

Everything inside me stopped, my mind went into sleep mode, and suddenly I didn't care about anything. I went back to Chloe, and we took a cab to her place. We had sex—this time without the picture of her ex-boyfriend on the wall. Afterward, she went to the kitchen and brought a bottle of whiskey back to bed, which we drank until we fell asleep.

12

The next morning I had a small hangover, and I came into the office late. Nicky was emptying her stuff from her desk and was ready to go to the airport and her new chase for success. We said good-bye and hugged. I wished her luck and said I'd visit her when I was in NYC next.

I walked to the cafeteria for a delayed morning coffee with Daniel, who was late to the office as well. Daniel made two cups, and we sat down by one of the tables. He said that he went home with a girl last night and didn't sleep much because she was constantly talking. I didn't tell him that I went home with Chloe. I felt guilty for some reason.

"So Nicky is on her way," Daniel said, setting his mug on the table.

"Yeah, good for her to try a new role."

"She's been working hard," he said, "like the fucking Duracell Bunny."

"It's a chase. Everyone wants to become the big fat cat eating caviar in a castle overlooking a vineyard." I sipped my drink.

Daniel glanced out the window. "I know, the rat race goes on and the only thing people seem to care about is getting promoted, and once they do, they want to get promoted again. Feels like I'm silently dying on the phone pitching stuff. Doesn't really seem to be a point to it. How do you manage to wake up every day, go to work, and not think about it? Or do you?"

"The only thing I'm thinking about these days is getting the fuck out of here."

"Not sure how you feel, but it's like I'm supposed to be part of something great and something really cool. That is what my friends think, but in the meantime, I don't feel like I'm adding anything to the world. I guess I just need to dare to take the step to get the fuck out." He took a sip of his coffee and stared out the window and into the office building across the street.

He reminded me of the flight attendant who'd served me whiskey while looking like a sad clown on my flight to San Francisco last year.

Daniel continued, "It's comfortable to be here you know, to get paid, get the food, the in-office dentist, the gym. But you're a rat in the wheel, running without getting anywhere."

"It's a roller coaster, my friend—a factory." I shrugged. "It's the industrial revolution happening again, just with different tools."

"Why do people like it? Why do they keep doing it?"

"The brand. It's cool. You get a satisfaction most people don't when you answer the question about where you work. And the food." I gestured at the kitchen. "Basic needs, like animals. Like you said, you feel too comfortable to leave. Everything is taken care of. You don't need to think or worry. You just have to work and obey."

"Yeah, maybe, I guess. When I complain about something, Louise just says it's even worse at other companies, that this is the best you can get. To be honest, I like that you're thinking of getting out, but it's also a big gamble, isn't it?"

"Sure, but a gamble with what? I would say it's a bigger gamble to sit trapped and be miserable for years, maybe for life." I met his eyes. "That's a fucking gamble. If you try something else, at least you have a chance of a big fucking win."

"Success is measured by the amount of money you earn now-adays, right?" Daniel said.

I shook my head. "Not for me. It's different for everyone. Success is individual. As long as you feel successful yourself, you are successful. Having that feeling is a skill."

"That's true. Never thought about that."

"At the end of the day, nobody cares what you do, how much you make, where you live, or who you fuck. Everyone thinks of themselves and pays no attention to others. So don't worry."

"I have to admit something." Daniel seemed embarrassed. "I did coke the last week of the previous quarter. For the first time. I feel like a fucking loser."

"Seriously?"

"I was working late. Alex came by my desk. One thing led to another."

"Don't fucking ever do that again. You don't need that." I stood up and left.

Fucking Alex, fucking cokehead. I never thought Daniel would do it. Fucking drug lords. The phone call I got from John's mother after he OD'd played through my head as I stormed back to my desk.

As I passed Nicky's desk, I thought for a brief moment that she was still sitting at it. Then I realized it was someone else. In the quarter of an hour I'd been talking with Daniel she had been replaced by a new girl. It was like she'd never existed, even though I'd hugged her right there on the very same spot fifteen minutes before. It was still the same desk, the same screen, and the same phone. They'd replaced her like batteries in a remote. They replaced one brick in the game with a new one, a fresh clown for an old one, anything to keep the monkeys working and the circus growing.

I was scared of being just a number in a factory, scared of being exchanged and forgotten. I couldn't let that happen.

13

The steak I was chewing felt like plastic, the mashed potatoes tasted like soft rubber, and the vegetables didn't contribute any flavor at all: they were just dead. I'd started to see every benefit at work, even lunch, as a tool to keep me in the hamster wheel.

The desire for more couldn't be satisfied anymore. I had reached my tipping point, and the emotional roller coaster I'd been riding for the last couple of months was now going downhill, fast.

Why wasn't I happier? Why wasn't everyone else happier? Why were so many employees in line for the psychologist? Why were the best minds of my generation being destroyed and beginning to lose their shine and passion?

I didn't want to wake up when I was sixty and feel useless— even less did I want to wake up knowing that I'd missed out on all my dreams. The essence of dreams is that they are not real. The day you reach one, it turns into reality, and you then find a new one. You have to keep chasing new ambitions, over and over. That's how your life progresses and grows. Without something to work toward, we're just empty robots. Dreams give us meaning. They give us satisfaction while we chase them and pleasure once we reach them.

I had reached what I thought was my dream by working at SHOW. Now it was a reality that I had created, and it turned out it had never been my idea. Daniel had made me believe it was mine; I'd hitched a ride on his ambitions and made them my own, following what I thought was the definition of success. I knew I had to begin chasing new dreams or else I would continue to go down this path and feel useless.

Paths have fascinated me since childhood. People walk one after another to create them. We choose the same routes, the same directions. One person leads, the rest follow. The road is born, and it's not a revolution anymore—it's just an ordinary avenue, a standard. But we need fresh tracks, and for those we need people to step off the highway and take a risk, to start the trail that will later become the standard.

I didn't want to walk on the same path anymore. I didn't want to follow others and do what the magazines said I should do to call myself successful. I wanted to go my own way.

14

It was Thursday morning, and I felt like God. I had no burden on my shoulders, no anxiety, nothing but pure joy. I had breakfast at Magnolia before I went to the office: scrambled eggs with avocado and a cappuccino.

I entered the office with a big smile and walked up to my manager, Louise, and asked if she had five minutes to talk. She was sitting at her desk, hitting her keyboard, surrounded by Coke cans and Oreo cookies.

We went to a meeting room and sat down. I told her that I was out, that my gig was up. I was done. She didn't understand what I was talking about. I put my resignation letter on the table in front of her.

"You're resigning? I'm sorry to hear it, although I'd anticipated it. You've been very mentally absent lately."

"I have, and now you know why."

She didn't ask any questions. I knew she didn't care: I was just a number that would be replaced. An excited and passionate person would take my desk. I would soon be forgotten. I decided I wouldn't let that happen.

When I got back to my desk, I took my keys out of my pocket and carved my name on the side of the wooden desk: *V. Janoski*.

I was excited. The fire inside me was back.

15

No one at the office believed me. My colleagues couldn't accept that I would just resign from SHOW and leave corporate heaven, the best place in the world to work.

I had no plan and no job, but I had my freedom and dreams. Emancipated from the modern industrial life of corporate America, my mining days were over. I had left the moneymaking factory.

I told myself it was time to chase a new dream, the last one. I knew it was a lie. There is never a last one. There will always be one more, over and over again until you die. You can't have everything. If you have everything, you've got nothing to lose. And if you have nothing to lose, there's no reason to live.

Now that I was free, maybe I'd go to New York for a while to get to know my father. It was about time. Maybe I would kiss Maggie the next chance I got. Maybe I would write lyrics for Chris's band. I decided to do it all.

So I did.

ABOUT THE AUTHOR

Filip Syta is a former Google employee who chose to leave the tech world behind to satisfy his constant urge to write and to pursue his ambition of becoming a novelist. He was born and raised in Stockholm, Sweden. In 2011, he graduated with a master's degree in entrepreneurship from Lund University, Lund, Sweden. He aspires to make readers identify the truly important things in life.

LIST OF PATRONS

This book was made possible in part by the following grand patrons who preordered the book on Inkshares.com. Thank you.

Andréa Blomgren
Charlotte Rosenlind
Christopher Brixen
Cristopher Benitah
Daniel August Fritzman
Daniel Losinski
Gabriel Persson
Göran Sandberg
Henrik Haegermark

Jedrzej Szczesniak
Kacper S.
Malgorzata Daniszewska
Maria Karlsson
Maria Mackiewicz
Peter Carlsson
Prashant Søegaard
Sebastian Dannegard

INKSHARES